Mandie Mysteries

1. *Mandie and the Secret Tunnel*
2. *Mandie and the Cherokee Legend*
3. *Mandie and the Ghost Bandits*
4. *Mandie and the Forbidden Attic*
5. *Mandie and the Trunk's Secret*
6. *Mandie and the Medicine Man*
7. *Mandie and the Charleston Phantom*
8. *Mandie and the Abandoned Mine*
9. *Mandie and the Hidden Treasure*
10. *Mandie and the Mysterious Bells*
11. *Mandie and the Holiday Surprise*
12. *Mandie and the Washington Nightmare*
13. *Mandie and the Midnight Journey*
14. *Mandie and the Shipboard Mystery*
15. *Mandie and the Foreign Spies*
16. *Mandie and the Silent Catacombs*
17. *Mandie and the Singing Chalet*
18. *Mandie and the Jumping Juniper*
19. *Mandie and the Mysterious Fisherman*
20. *Mandie and the Windmill's Message*
21. *Mandie and the Fiery Rescue*

———

Mandie's Cookbook

MANDIE
AND THE
WINDMILL'S MESSAGE

Lois Gladys Leppard

BETHANY HOUSE PUBLISHERS

MINNEAPOLIS, MINNESOTA 55438

A Ministry of Bethany Fellowship, Inc.

Mandie and the Windmill's Message
Lois Gladys Leppard

All scripture quotations are taken from the
King James Version of the Bible.

Library of Congress Catalog Card Number 92–73061

ISBN 1–55661–288–5

Published by Bethany House Publishers
A Ministry of Bethany Fellowship, Inc.
6820 Auto Club Road, Minneapolis, Minnesota 55438

Printed in the United States of America

For J. Robert and Sarah O. Ritter,

Dear Friends and Advisers,

With Thanks.

About the Author

LOIS GLADYS LEPPARD has been a Federal Civil Service employee in various countries around the world. She makes her home in Greenville, South Carolina.

The stories of her own mother's childhood are the basis for many of the incidents incorporated in this series.

Contents

"But if ye do not forgive, neither will your Father which is in heaven forgive your trespasses."

Mark 11:26

Chapter 1 / Questions in Holland

"I hear music!" Mandie Shaw exclaimed. She quickly turned to look all around from the carriage in which she and her friends, Celia Hamilton and Jonathan Guyer, were traveling in Holland.

Her grandmother, Mrs. Taft, and their family friend, Senator Morton, sat across from them. The adults turned and smiled as the young people searched for a glimpse of the source of the music.

"It's probably a parade, from the sound of it, dear," Mrs. Taft told Mandie.

"A parade!" Celia said, pushing back her long auburn hair under the bonnet she was wearing.

"It probably is a parade," Jonathan spoke up. "This is flower season in Holland and they have lots of flower parades."

"How do you know?" Mandie asked as she glanced at him.

Jonathan smiled at her and said, "You forget. First of

all, this is the country of my ancestors. And I have also been to school in this country."

"Sorry, I keep forgetting you are so well-traveled," Mandie teased as she held on to her white kitten, Snowball, who was awake now and trying to get out of her lap.

"Well, when you get back home to North Carolina, you will also be able to say you are well-traveled, at least for a thirteen-year-old girl," Jonathan told her with his mischievous grin.

Just as Mandie opened her mouth to reply, Celia excitedly pointed outside. "There it is. It *is* a parade. Oh, all those beautiful flowers!" she exclaimed.

Mandie quickly looked over at the spectacle on the road that crossed theirs just ahead. She glanced back at Jonathan and said, "You were actually right." Pushing close to Celia at the window, she said, "I've never in my life seen so many flowers. And so many colors, too. Everything seems to be made out of flowers. Those carts and the ponies pulling them are just covered. And look, even the people in it are wearing whole blankets of flowers. I wonder how they get the flowers to stay together?"

The driver of their carriage brought the vehicle to a halt at the intersection. To Mandie, the parade seemed to be miles long.

"Grandmother, could we just get out while we're stopped so we can smell the flowers?" Mandie asked Mrs. Taft.

"Yes, that would be a good idea. We'll all just stand outside and stretch our legs," Mrs. Taft told her.

Jonathan was already opening the door and helping the girls down as Senator Morton rose to assist Mrs. Taft. The young people rushed forward to stand as near as they could get without interfering with the progress of the parade.

Mandie smiled at the people walking in the parade, but she realized they were looking straight ahead without a glance in her direction. She waved, but the participants still wouldn't acknowledge her presence.

"Oh, I can't get anyone to look at me," Mandie said with a sigh.

"Why do you want them to look at you? They have to keep step and watch where they're going," Jonathan said, then added, "They can probably tell we're nobody important."

"Jonathan, you don't have to be important to say hello to somebody," Mandie protested as she continued to wave.

Mrs. Taft and Senator Morton walked up behind the young people. "Permit me to explain, Miss Amanda," Senator Morton said, with a smile at Jonathan. "Those people can't wave or turn their heads because they are weighted down with flowers all over their bodies. If they made a wrong movement they'd probably tear some of the flowers loose."

"Oh," Mandie said, dropping her arm. "I understand. I won't wave, then. I don't want to cause them to damage something." She watched as the parade continued by.

"I'm sure they won't mind if you want to wave, dear," Mrs. Taft said, "even though they can't wave back."

At that moment, a full band came into view playing a lively march. The musicians walked faster and urged the pony carts on. The three young people clapped to the music as they watched.

Without interrupting her clapping, Mandie looked up at her grandmother and said, "The musicians have so many flowers on them and their instruments, I don't see how they can play."

"They're experienced. There are so many flower parades in this country, I imagine these people are in more than one parade," Mrs. Taft explained.

"Oh, Mandie, did you see that man with the horn blow off a rose?" Celia asked, pointing to where the flower fell by the road.

Mandie rushed forward, snatched up the rose, and moved back to the side of the road. She smelled its fragrance and touched the velvet petals as Snowball squirmed in her arms.

"I'll press this and take it home with me," Mandie said.

"The end seems to be coming up. Shall we return to the carriage?" Senator Morton asked Mrs. Taft as the last figures came into sight.

"Yes, we should be hurrying on so we can get to the house before dark," Mrs. Taft said, turning back toward the waiting carriage. "Come along, Amanda, Celia, Jonathan."

As they all took their seats in the vehicle, Mandie asked, "This house we're going to be staying in, will there be other people there?"

"No, dear, only the servants. We rented it from a family who had it listed with a real-estate agency. They are all away for the summer," Mrs. Taft explained.

"I hope it's not too big and spooky like the one in Switzerland," Mandie told her.

"It's not that big," her grandmother said. "There are bedrooms for all of us and one for Uncle Ned when he comes."

Uncle Ned was Mandie's father's Cherokee friend. When Jim Shaw died, the old Indian had promised to watch over Mandie. He had even journeyed to Europe in order to keep his promise. But he seemed to have acquaintances all over the world, and was always going off somewhere to visit someone.

"Uncle Ned promised he would spend more time with us in Holland than he has in all the other countries we've visited," Mandie said, holding the bright red rose she had picked up. Just as the driver started off with the vehicle, Mandie looked down the road at the end of the parade still in sight. "They sure are marching awfully slow at the end of the line," she remarked.

Celia and Jonathan looked out the window. At that moment, two figures broke away from the marching column and ran back the way they had come.

"Look, they're leaving the parade!" Mandie exclaimed, watching them come closer.

"Maybe they live around here someplace," Jonathan said.

As the two participants came nearer, Mandie got a look at their faces. One was a beautiful blonde girl and the other was a handsome dark fellow. They kept looking back at the parade disappearing in the distance as they ran. The carriage approached the intersection, and they hurried past without a glance at the vehicle. The driver had to slow the horses to keep from hitting them.

"She was pretty, wasn't she?" Celia remarked.

"And he was good-looking," Mandie added with a smile. She laid the rose in her lap, and tied Snowball's leash to the door handle. Then she pulled her journal and a pencil out of a bag at her feet. "I think I'll press this rose in my diary," she said, opening the book to a blank page. She inserted the rose and pressed the book closed, holding it firmly in her lap.

"Are you going to record our journey from Belgium to Holland?" Celia asked as she took her journal and pencil from her bag.

"I suppose so," Mandie said. "But I'm going to run out of paper for 1901 if I keep writing about *everything* we see and do. I think I'll have to stay home next year and catch up on other things." She pushed her long, blonde braid under her bonnet, and her blue eyes turned thoughtful as she opened the book to begin writing.

"You girls had better not let that Miss Prudence, or whatever her name is at your school in Asheville, find out you've done all this writing," Jonathan teased. "She'll be having you read it to your class."

"Never!" Mandie said, scribbling away in her book. "No one is ever going to read what I write in this diary."

"Nor mine," Celia added.

"No one?" Jonathan questioned Mandie with a grin. "Not even that Joe fellow who wants to marry you when the two of you grow up?"

Mandie frowned and gave him a stern look. "Not even him. No one."

"About ten years from now I'll ask you again about that diary," Jonathan said, still grinning.

"I doubt that I'll see you around ten years from now. You'll be grown and married," Mandie said, without looking up from her writing.

"And where will you be in 1911? Probably married to that Joe back home," Jonathan teased.

"Jonathan Guyer—" Mandie began loudly.

"Amanda," Mrs. Taft interrupted. "What are you arguing about?"

Mandie looked at her grandmother's stern face and replied, "Nothing really, Grandmother. I'm sorry if I disturbed you. I was just writing in my journal."

"I apologize, Mrs. Taft," Jonathan said. "I was only teasing Mandie, and I suppose we were talking too loud."

"We'll soon be to the house where we'll be staying," Mrs. Taft told them. "Then you can go outside and argue to your hearts' content."

"Yes, Grandmother," Mandie said. She put her journal and the pencil back into the bag, and straightened up to watch the scenery through the carriage window. Turning back to her friends, she sighed and said, "I wonder who those people were that we saw leave the parade. They were acting mysteriously."

"Oh, Mandie, you always see a mystery in everything," Celia said. "I didn't see anything mysterious about those people."

"Well, I can imagine, can't I? Besides, Uncle Ned told us we would find another mystery in Holland," Mandie said.

"I think he said that because he knows you always find an adventure everywhere you go," Jonathan said.

"And you always join in," Mandie reminded him as she moved her feet from where Snowball was sleeping. She suddenly straightened up and exclaimed, "Look! Real windmills!" She pointed to two large windmills standing in a distant field full of blooming purple flowers.

Jonathan and Celia crowded close to the window to look. "The blades are set for celebration," Jonathan said.

"What do you mean?" Mandie asked.

"The people in this country use windmill blades for signals," he explained. "When the blades are stationary and set with the top blade just before what would be twelve o'clock, like those out there, that means a celebration is going on—probably the rose parade we just saw."

"Are there other signals?" Celia asked.

"When the top blade is stopped right past the twelve o'clock mark, that is an indication of mourning. And when the blades are set at three, six, nine, and twelve o'clock positions, the miller is resting for a short period. When set at one-thirty, four-thirty, seven-thirty, and ten-thirty, the miller is resting for a longer period of time," the boy replied.

"That's interesting. Are there more?" Mandie asked.

"That's all I know," Jonathan said. "Besides, I don't see how there could be more positions. The four blades move together, you know."

"Do the people here really wear wooden shoes?" Mandie asked.

"Sometimes," Jonathan said. "Most of the time they wear shoes like everybody else, but the wooden shoes are part of their history. I had a pair once, but my feet got too big for them." He laughed.

"I want to buy a pair to take home," Mandie said, and then with a grin she added, "I might even wear them to school."

"Mandie! You wouldn't!" Celia exclaimed.

"Why not?" Mandie asked.

"Because I don't think they would be comfortable. And besides, they'd probably be awfully noisy, and Miss Prudence wouldn't stand for that," Celia told her.

"Well, I wouldn't wear them all the time," Mandie said.

The young people had been talking and not paying any attention to the scenery. As a small house came into view, Mrs. Taft drew their attention to it. "That is the house," she said, pointing to it.

The three anxiously looked through the carriage window. It was a small house—quaint, and different from any they'd seen in the other countries. It was surrounded with flowers and willow trees. There didn't seem to be any other structures nearby.

"It's built so low to the ground it looks like it has grown tired and just hunkered down," Mandie said with a laugh as Snowball jumped into her lap.

The others laughed with her, and the adults smiled.

The driver pulled up in front of the house and jumped down to open the door of the carriage.

"This is it, madam," the man said as he offered Mrs. Taft his hand to assist her from the vehicle.

Senator Morton followed and the young people sprang out behind him.

Mrs. Taft stood still, looking puzzled. "I don't see anyone. Surely the servants will come out and get our bags," she said.

They all remained where they were for a moment, and finally Senator Morton said, "I'll just go to the door." He quickly walked up the short pathway.

Everyone watched while he knocked on the door. No one came outside.

"Jonathan," the senator called to him. "I know you are fluent in Dutch. Would you come here and call out that we have arrived—just in case the people don't speak English."

"Yes, sir," the boy replied as he hurried to join the senator. Mandie and Celia watched with Mrs. Taft as Jonathan knocked heavily on the door and called out in Dutch.

Between the knocks and the calling there was complete silence. The sun was rapidly going down, and Mandie realized it must be near suppertime. Snowball stretched at the end of his red leash. The driver stood, waiting for someone to unload the baggage.

Mrs. Taft quickly walked up the pathway, followed by the girls. "Don't tell me there's no one here," she said crossly.

"I'll check the back, Mrs. Taft," Jonathan offered.

"You go around that way and I'll go around this side," Senator Morton told him. "We'll meet at the back door."

As they disappeared around each side of the house,

Mrs. Taft spoke to the girls, "I do hope this is the right house."

The driver overheard her and said, "Yes, madam, this is the house. I know the fellow who drives for these people. Their name is van Courtland, isn't that correct? And they have gone on holiday."

"Yes, that's right," Mrs. Taft agreed. "When the real estate agency engaged the house for us and arranged for you to bring us here, I had no idea you knew the family. Then tell me, where are the servants?"

"They would be with the family, except for the cook, one maid, and the manservant," the driver explained.

"Well, it doesn't look like anyone is here at all," Mrs. Taft said as she looked around again. "Thank goodness we have engaged you and your carriage for our stay here."

"Maybe we came on the wrong date," Mandie suggested.

"No, dear, the real estate agency confirmed our reservation for the house," Mrs. Taft said.

"Then maybe the servants got the date mixed up and went off somewhere," Mandie guessed.

"That's possible," her grandmother replied.

"But highly unlikely that all the servants would leave the house at the same time," the driver said, standing by the horses that were becoming restless.

Celia spoke to the driver. "Mr. . . . er . . . uh, I'm afraid I don't know your name . . ."

"William, miss," the driver told her.

Celia smiled at him and said, "Mr. William, are there other people living around here? I don't see any other houses."

"Certainly, miss," William said. "Just a stone's throw to the east there is a lovely widow and her son, and to the west there is the miller and his family. You would have to go around back in order to see the windmill."

"A windmill! Come on, Celia, we have to go look!" Mandie said excitedly, picking up Snowball.

"Wait, not so fast," Mrs. Taft told her. "I am going with you to see what is keeping the senator and Jonathan so long." Turning back to the driver, she said, "William, wait here, please. We'll be right back."

"Yes, madam," he said.

The girls and Mrs. Taft went around the side of the house where Senator Morton had gone. The pathway was covered with cobblestones, and the sweet scent of red roses growing along the way floated around them as their long skirts swished the air. The house did seem to be "hunkering down," as Mandie had said. The windows opened almost to the ground and the roof hung low. Evidently its stone walls were old but well-kept. And it was much larger than it had looked from the front.

"Senator Morton," Mrs. Taft called as they rounded the corner to the back yard. "Jonathan."

No one answered. Mandie ran ahead when they finally spotted the back door, but the senator and Jonathan were nowhere to be seen.

Mandie paused before the door and waited for her grandmother and Celia. "I don't see them anywhere," Mandie said.

Mrs. Taft quickly looked around. "Perhaps they went inside."

She started toward the closed door and then paused as Mandie said, "No, Grandmother. I see them coming through the yard there."

The three of them waited as Senator Morton and Jonathan came toward them from the direction of a barn that was set a great distance back in the yard.

"Sorry, but there doesn't seem to be anyone around," Senator Morton told them.

"Not even in the barn," Jonathan added.

"Oh, goodness, what will we do?" Mrs. Taft exclaimed. "Something has obviously gone wrong with our plans."

"Well, did you try the door to see if it's locked?" Mandie asked, turning back.

"No, we didn't," Senator Morton said. "No one came when we knocked."

Mandie reached for the door handle, and at her touch the door slowly swung inward. The smell of freshly baked bread reached her nostrils. There was a sudden rattling of iron pans as she tried to see inside the dark room. Then a large cat came hurtling out, growling as he passed Snowball on his leash. A loud bang seemed to shake the house. Mandie jumped back in fright and stumbled over Celia, who was directly behind her.

Mandie steadied herself and said in a hoarse whisper, "There's somebody in there!"

Chapter 2 / She Can't Hear, and He
Can't Speak

Even the adults froze as the racket in the room continued. Mrs. Taft reached for the senator's arm, and he
held her hand. When Mandie stepped backward, Celia
grasped her by the skirt, and Jonathan put an arm around
both the girls to steady them when they collided.

Suddenly there was complete silence in the room,
and the young people cautiously moved forward to peek
inside. They heard a woman's voice humming a song,
softly at first, then building to high-pitched, off-key notes.

Mandie whispered to her friends, "Let's see who's in
there." She stepped through the doorway. Jonathan and
Celia followed. Once inside, Mandie could see that it was
a large kitchen illuminated only by the failing light of day
through several windows. In the far corner she spied an
old woman busily stirring something in a large bowl on
a table.

"Pardon me, ma'am, but we couldn't get anyone to

the door," Mandie said, slowly approaching the woman. She was wearing an old mobcap and a flowing white apron over a severe black dress. There was no response. Mandie moved nearer and spoke again, "Ma'am, we are the people who have rented this place—" she began.

Mrs. Taft interrupted as she hurried toward the old woman. "Amanda, I'll take care of it." As she finally stood in front of the woman, she was able to get her attention. The servant looked up, smiled at Mrs. Taft, and went on with her work.

"I am Mrs. Taft. We've rented this place while the own-ers are on vacation," Mandie's grandmother tried to ex-plain to the woman. But she continued stirring the con-tents of the bowl and ignored her.

Mrs. Taft looked up at Senator Morton. "What do you think is wrong?" Mrs. Taft asked him in a low voice.

"I believe the woman must be deaf. That would ex-plain all the noise. She can't hear what she's doing," Sen-ator Morton said. Then walking nearer to the woman he stopped in front of her, touched her on the shoulder and began making signs with his hands and his face. He tried to explain who they were.

The woman watched intently and then suddenly reached for a heavy rope hanging near the stove. She pulled on it, and a loud bell rang outside.

The young people listened and watched. Suddenly a tall, husky man rushed through the doorway and looked around the room. When he saw Mrs. Taft and the others, he stopped and stared.

Senator Morton spoke up. "We are the Americans who have rented this place while the owners are on va-cation. I assume you work here. We haven't been able to get anyone to the door, and the lady here evidently can't hear us," he said.

The man smiled and nodded his head. He pointed to her ears and nodded in the affirmative. Then he pointed to his own mouth and shook his head.

"I think I understand what you mean. You can hear, but you can't speak, is that correct?" the senator asked.

The man smiled again and nodded in the affirmative. Then he made signs to the senator that he was going out for their luggage. Senator Morton went with him.

As they left the room, Mandie said, "The lady can't hear and the man can't talk. Well, I suppose they fill in for each other, but how are we going to communicate with them?"

"I will take care of that, miss," a woman's voice said behind her, and she turned to see another woman, younger than the first, coming into the kitchen. She had her arms full of bundles, which she dumped onto the large table at the end of the long room. Evidently, she had been shopping.

"Thank goodness for someone who can speak," Mrs. Taft said.

"Madam, I am Gretchen, the maid. I will show you to your rooms," the girl said, straightening her black uniform, and adjusting the tiny white cap on top of her thick blonde hair. "And anything that you and your party need, just ask me. I know how to communicate with Anna, the cook." She turned, touched the old woman on the shoulder, and began using sign language and mouthing words. The woman responded in the same way and then smiled at Mrs. Taft.

"Oh, I'd like to learn to do that," Mandie commented.

"Me, too," Celia said.

"It is not hard to learn, but Anna does not understand English. You would have to learn in Dutch," Gretchen said.

"Does sign language vary for the different languages?" Jonathan asked.

"I am not sure, but I also form words with my lips to help her to understand," Gretchen said. "Now, if you will come with me . . . Dieter must have your luggage in your rooms by now. And Anna will have your meal ready within the hour."

The house only had two stories and was not huge like the other places in which they had stayed on their journey through Europe. Mandie, Celia, and Jonathan took in every detail as they went along the corridors. Gretchen first showed Mrs. Taft her rooms, which consisted of a small sitting room and a large bedroom. "The gentleman will be in the rooms next-door to madam," Gretchen told Mrs. Taft.

At that moment, Senator Morton came out of the next room. "We've finished bringing in all the luggage," he said. William and Dieter followed him out into the hallway.

"I will be taking a room in the barn, madam," William said. "If you need me, all you have to do is send the maid." He bowed slightly and turned to walk down the corridor.

Dieter smiled and followed him.

"Now, you, misses, will have a room together at the end of the hallway." Gretchen pointed to her left as she spoke. "And you, young man, will have a room at the other end of the hallway." She pointed to her right.

Mandie and Celia quickly inspected the room the maid had showed them.

"At least we have a bathroom. Snowball needs that when we go out and leave him," Mandie remarked as she held tightly to the white kitten. Turning to Gretchen she asked, "Would it be possible for the manservant to get a box of sand and put it in our bathroom for Snowball?"

"Of course, miss. We did not know you would be

bringing an animal," Gretchen said, smiling. "I will have that done immediately." She left to take care of it.

Once the door was shut, Mandie let Snowball down, and he roamed the room. She went to the heavy draperies and pulled them back to look outside. The girls were in a corner room with windows on both sides.

"Celia, look! I can see the windmill that William must have been talking about. Way over there. See it?" she said, pointing across the fields behind the house. The blades of the windmill were barely visible in the distance.

"Maybe we could go over for a closer look," Celia suggested as she leaned forward and squinted her eyes.

"William said the miller and his family live to the west, by the windmill, remember?" Mandie said. "And a widow and her son live to the east. I don't think we can see the east side from here. If we are on the west side of the house, then Jonathan would be on the east. We'll have to ask him if he can see the lady's house."

"Right now we'd better clean up and change clothes," Celia reminded her as she went to her trunk, unlocked it, and lifted the lid. "I'm going to hang up some of these clothes so they won't be so wrinkled." She took out dresses and hung them in the huge wardrobe.

"I guess I'd better hang my dresses, too," Mandie said. As she quickly hung each one, she said, "I still wonder where that girl and young man who left the parade went."

"Mandie, I don't imagine we'll ever find that out," Celia said, slipping out of her traveling suit and pulling on a fresh, green voile dress. "We don't even know who they were."

"Well, you never know," Mandie replied as she buttoned up her pale blue dress. "I know Grandmother will take us sightseeing here, because she always does wherever we go. We might just run into them somewhere. I would know their faces if I saw them again."

The evening meal was served in a dining room that was about half the size of other places they had dined. Mandie looked around the table. It was still not as small as their dining room back home, but it was much more comfortable than the huge rooms they'd been in while in other countries.

"I think I'm going to like Holland," Mandie remarked as Gretchen began serving the meal. "I feel more at home here."

"Well, yes, I suppose you would," Mrs. Taft replied from the end of the table. "But, remember, we are in the country. This is a country house. There are much more impressive places in the cities." She turned back to converse with Senator Morton.

Mandie leaned toward Jonathan across the table and asked in a low voice, "Can you see the widow lady's house, that William told us about, from your window? We saw the windmill and the place where the miller lives from ours."

Jonathan nodded. "I saw a small cottage way off in the distance. I suppose that's the one William referred to," Jonathan told her. Then he asked, "Did you notice what position the windmill blades were in?"

"Oh, shucks," Mandie said with a sigh. "I forgot all about that. But I'll look when we go back to our room." She looked at her grandmother, who was deep in conversation with the senator. "And as soon as we get a chance, I'd like to go down there and look at it." She took a bite of the freshly baked bread.

Celia spoke up. "Your grandmother will take us sightseeing and we can see lots of windmills then."

"But that's not the same. We're practically living on the same property as the windmill," Mandie said.

"Be sure to look every chance you get to see what position the blades are in. Just tell me, and I'll help you interpret what they mean," Jonathan said.

"Do you think we could visit the miller and his family and get him to show us the windmill?" Mandie asked, laying down her fork.

"With or without your grandmother?" Jonathan teased.

"Well, you know, if we went by ourselves—" Mandie began.

Mrs. Taft interrupted, "Went where by yourselves, Amanda?"

Mandie felt a flush come over her face. She had thought her grandmother was absorbed in conversation with Senator Morton. She tried to explain. "You know that windmill near the home of the miller and his family that William told us about? Well, we can see it from our bedroom window, and we thought if you and Senator Morton were too busy, we could go over there by ourselves and see it," she said all in a rush.

"We'll see about that," Mrs. Taft said. "I do want you girls to see and learn everything you can about this country. I know Jonathan has lived here, and is well-informed because his ancestors came from here. But, Amanda, did I ever tell you that you are a descendant from a Pilgrim who sailed from Delfshaven Port not far from here? I intend to take you all over there."

Mandie's blue eyes lit with excitement as she replied, "But, Grandmother, how could that be? I've never heard that before."

"You are descended through my mother's family from way back, several great, great, great—offhand I can't remember how many—grandmothers to the young Pilgrim girl who was our ancestor," Mrs. Taft explained, and then added quickly, "You and I need to spend a lot more time together when we get back to North Carolina. There are lots of things I would like you to know about the family, things that your mother could care less about. I think you will someday write our family history." She smiled at Mandie.

"Me? Write the family history? But, Grandmother, I wouldn't know how to begin such a thing," Mandie said in surprise.

"All you have to do is write down everything you see, hear, or read about our family. That will be a good beginning," Mrs. Taft replied. She turned back to the senator.

"Sounds like an awfully big job," Mandie said, looking at her friends.

"Not really," Jonathan said. "I know people who have compiled our family history, and they work just as your grandmother said—recording everything." He paused, then grinned as he said, "With your nose for mystery, I think you'd be great at it." He took a sip of his hot tea.

"Jonathan, I do not have a *nose* for mystery," Mandie told him curtly. "I have an analytical mind." She drummed on her glass with her fingers.

"Whatever you call it, Mandie, I agree with Jonathan that you'd be good at it," Celia told her around a mouthful of potatoes.

"And just think of all those family skeletons you'll find. You'll know all the family secrets," Jonathan teased.

"Family skeletons? In the graveyard?" Mandie asked.

"No. Family skeletons are things that the family would like to keep hidden—maybe a bad deed someone has done, or an illegitimate child, or even a murder, maybe," Jonathan told her.

"A murder?" Mandie was shocked. "In our family?"

"Now, I didn't say there *was* one in your family," Jonathan quickly responded. "But some people do uncover such things when tracing their ancestors."

"Well, I don't think I'll be tracing my ancestors. I know my Cherokee kinpeople and that's all I care about," Mandie said. "Jonathan, do you have any relatives here in Holland?" She began eating the fish on her plate.

"Oh, no, they're all dead. Our family came to the United States over a hundred years ago," Jonathan explained. He took a bite of bread and washed it down with more tea. "This bread is absolutely the best I've had in Europe."

"I agree," Celia said, eating a piece herself.

Mrs. Taft spoke from the end of the table, "How about less talk and more eating? I'd like to go for a walk as soon as we're finished."

"Yes, ma'am," the three chorused as they quickly cleaned off their plates.

After they had finished the meal, Mrs. Taft and Senator Morton led the way down narrow lanes that wound through the fields full of colorful flowers and shrubs toward the widow's cottage. The three young people followed, bending now and then to smell or admire a particular flower.

"I do wish Grandmother had gone in the direction of the windmill," Mandie said to her friends. Snowball walked along at the end of his red leash.

"But, Mandie, it will be dark soon. We'll see it tomorrow in the daylight," Celia reminded her.

"We could at least have had a closer glimpse of it," Mandie replied.

"Has your grandmother made plans for tomorrow yet?" Jonathan asked.

"I don't know," Mandie said. "She mentioned the Delfshaven Port at the table tonight, you know, and I remember hearing her say something while we were in Belgium about the Delftware factory here."

"They both sound like interesting places," Celia said as they trailed along.

"At least more interesting than those stuffy old museums we always have to visit," Jonathan said with a smile.

"Don't count on it. We may still have to visit another one," Mandie said. "As far as I am concerned, I don't give a flip for all those antique paintings done by people who died so many years ago. I'm more interested in the here and now, and the future."

"But Mrs. Taft was nice enough to bring us on this journey to Europe, so we have to go wherever she wants to," Celia reminded the other two.

"Now wait a minute. She didn't bring me to Europe," Jonathan corrected her. "I came on my own."

"But she agreed to take you with us until your father comes to get you. Besides, when we met up with you, you were on one of *her* ships, remember?" Mandie said.

Jonathan smiled and said, "I know. I owe her a lot. I do hope my aunt and uncle in Paris stay home there long enough for me to visit them when you all go back to the United States."

Mandie suddenly stopped and squinted. There was someone walking through the flowers a long way ahead.

"Look! I see someone up ahead," she told her friends, pointing.

Celia and Jonathan paused to look.

"Well, what's so unusual about that?" Jonathan asked.

"He's coming this way," Mandie said, excitedly walking on down the trail. Snowball tried to race ahead on his leash.

Mrs. Taft and Senator Morton were a long way ahead of them now, because the young people had stopped so often to examine the flowers and to talk.

Celia and Jonathan looked at each other and then followed Mandie. Mrs. Taft turned to glance back and motioned for them to come ahead.

As Mandie watched the figure, he seemed to zigzag across the field, sometimes coming toward them, and then turning the other way. Finally she was near enough to recognize the young man. He was as the one who had left the parade! She hurried toward him and raised her free hand to wave. The man stopped in surprise, took a good look at the three young people, and then turned and ran in the other direction.

Mandie stopped. "Now why did he run away?" she asked as she watched the figure disappear among the flowers.

"It was the man from the parade, wasn't it?" Celia asked as she stopped by Mandie's side.

"Yes, it was, and I can't figure out why he turned back the other way when he saw us," Mandie said, holding on to Snowball's leash. "He acted like he didn't want to get near us."

"Are you *sure* he was the man from the parade?" Jonathan asked.

"Yes, he was. Celia thought so too, didn't you, Celia?" Mandie asked.

"I'm positive," Celia replied.

"He's gone now," Jonathan said.

"He acted awfully strange. Maybe he didn't want us to see him for some reason, but I can't imagine why," Mandie said as the three walked on to catch up with the adults. "I'll have to think about that. Maybe we'll see him again."

Chapter 3 / Windmill Blades in the Wrong Position

They circled the fields and returned to the house as the sun slipped away. Mrs. Taft and Senator Morton walked ahead.

At the doorway, Mrs. Taft turned to say, "I think we should all go to our rooms and get some sleep. We will be going to Delfshaven Port tomorrow—and whatever else there is time for."

"Could we have a cup of tea before we retire?" Mandie asked as they entered the front door and stood by the open doorway to the parlor.

"You'd like some tea?" Mrs. Taft questioned with surprise. Mandie was a coffee drinker and usually spurned tea.

"Yes, ma'am," the three young people chorused.

Gretchen had entered the hallway and overheard their conversation. "Yes, yes, good idea! I will have some brewing for you. Sit in the parlor and I will be right back with it," she said with a big smile as she went through a doorway at the end of the hallway.

Mrs. Taft went on into the parlor and sat down. Senator Morton joined her on the small settee. The young people found seats around the room, which was furnished in bright blues. The Dutch look was so clean and crisp, Mandie thought. She looped the end of Snowball's leash around a chair leg and he curled up on the carpet to take a nap.

"I suppose it's a good idea to have some refreshment," Mrs. Taft said as she relaxed. "That was a rather tiring stroll through all those crooked pathways up and down the hills."

Mandie waited until her grandmother had become engrossed in conversation with the senator, and then she spoke in a low tone to her friends. "I am not one bit tired or sleepy. And if sleep doesn't overcome me when I go to our room, I may just go out for some fresh night air." She grinned.

"And go to see what the windmill looks like?" Jonathan asked with his mischievous grin.

"Oh, Mandie, you wouldn't!" Celia protested as she glanced at Mrs. Taft.

"Celia, you have no sense of adventure. We may never have this opportunity again," Mandie said in a mysterious tone.

"I'd like to go with you," Jonathan told her.

"I'll tap on your door if I decide to go," Mandie promised.

"Here we go again," Celia said with a sigh.

"We? Will you go, too?" Mandie asked in a whisper.

"If you do, I'll have to," Celia said with resignation. "You may need me for something."

Mandie smiled at her friend. "I always appreciate your help, Celia."

Jonathan leaned toward Mandie and asked softly, "Then are you really going? Because if you are, I won't bother to undress for the night, but will wait for you to tap on my door."

"Unless some earth-shaking problem comes up, I'll be ready about thirty minutes after we go to our rooms," Mandie declared.

At that moment, Gretchen wheeled in a tea cart laden with sweets and a large silver teapot. She went directly to Mrs. Taft, lifted off a silver tray, and set it on a nearby table. Then she laid out the china tea dishes.

"You are tempting me with all those delicious-looking desserts," Mrs. Taft remarked.

"Yes, madam," Gretchen said with a big smile. "And you must sample each one. I will leave the cart. Is there anything else?"

"Oh, no thank you, Gretchen. This is more than enough," Mrs. Taft told her.

The maid nodded and left the room.

As Mrs. Taft poured the tea and passed it around, she said to Mandie, "I really should let you do this for practice. You said they are teaching you how to pour out tea and serve the boys from Mr. Chadwick's school back home. Isn't that right?"

"Yes, Grandmother. But you do the honors. I've had plenty of practice already," Mandie said quickly. "Besides, I love to watch you. You are always a real lady in everything you do."

Mrs. Taft's face flushed at the compliment, and she replied, "Not always a lady, I'm afraid, my dear. I have trouble sometimes living up to society's expectations."

"Then you should only live up to your own expectations," Mandie told her as she sipped her tea.

Senator Morton spoke up. "You are right, Miss

Amanda. Your grandmother always conducts herself as a lady, no matter what she might say."

"Well, thank you, Senator Morton," Mrs. Taft managed, blushing again.

"And was my grandfather always a gentleman?" Mandie asked the senator.

"Yes, your grandfather was always the perfect gentleman—always. There was nothing anyone could fault him with," Senator Morton assured her.

"Well, then if both my grandparents are such gentle people, why isn't my mother like them?" Mandie asked.

"Your mother has always been just like your grandfather, dear, never veering to the left or right, but walking a straight line. I've always said she should have a little more spine about her and do some things differently from what's expected," Mrs. Taft said, reaching for a sweetcake.

Mandie's eyes widened, and she straightened her shoulders and jutted out her chin. "Then I must take after you, Grandmother, in all my reckless ways."

Everyone in the room laughed.

"I wouldn't call it reckless, Amanda. It's determination, dear," Mrs. Taft replied with a smile. "Yes, you are like me in many ways."

Mandie's mind stored this remark. It may come in handy later on, in case she ever got into trouble because of her "reckless ways."

After the tea was finished and good-nights were said, everyone went to their rooms. Mrs. Taft paused at her door to say, "Amanda, you and Celia should be up and dressed for breakfast at seven o'clock. You too, Jonathan. That's what time I asked Gretchen to have it ready."

"Yes, ma'am," the three chorused.

"Pleasant dreams now," Mrs. Taft said as she went into her suite.

"Thirty minutes," Mandie whispered to Jonathan as he turned down the hallway toward his room. He nodded and kept going.

Mandie and Celia flopped onto the bed in their room and watched the little china clock on the mantelpiece for thirty minutes to pass. Snowball curled up in a big chair and went to sleep.

"Mandie, do you not think it's wrong for us to do this?" Celia asked.

"Oh, Celia, after all, we're thirteen years old!" Mandie argued. "Besides, lots of girls are married when they're about three years older. Grandmother just doesn't realize we're growing up. And we aren't really doing anything *wrong*."

"Well, if you say so," Celia slowly replied. "Are we taking Snowball?"

"No, not tonight. He might get lost in the dark," Mandie said as she tossed back her long, blonde braid. "Celia, I know your mother, but I don't know her that well. Does she always walk a straight line, as my grandmother said my mother does?"

"Most of the time," Celia said, her green eyes becoming dreamy. "My Aunt Rebecca Hamilton is the exact opposite. My father was her brother, you know, and I suppose she is a lot like my father. He did a lot of unexpected things sometimes."

"So did my father," Mandie said. "And Uncle John is a lot like him. I'm so glad Uncle John married my mother after my father died." Her voice shook as she said it. She still missed her father so much.

"Do you think your little brother will be like them?" Celia asked.

"Oh, Samuel Hezekiah Shaw has a mind of his own. That's for sure. Remember I told you he cried all the time?" Mandie said with a laugh.

"But lots of newborn babies cry a lot, I've heard," Celia told her. "You are so lucky to have a brother. I wish I had a brother or sister."

"You can claim me for your sister," Mandie said with a smile. "I feel as though we are sisters, really." She sat up suddenly. "It's time to go!"

The girls tiptoed down the hallway and knocked lightly on Jonathan's door. He slipped out into the dimly-lit corridor to join them. Without uttering a word, the three went down the stairs and out the front door.

"This way," Mandie whispered as she turned in the direction of the windmill. Jonathan and Celia followed. No one said a word until they were well beyond hearing distance of the house.

"I think it's safe to talk now," Mandie said with a sigh. "We're getting closer. I can just barely see the windmill." She pointed ahead.

"I can, too," Jonathan said, and then he began walking faster. "I think the blades are at an odd position."

"They are?" Mandie questioned.

"Yes, they should be at one-thirty, four-thirty, seven-thirty, and ten-thirty positions this time of night, because the miller should be closed for the day," Jonathan explained as they hurried on through the field of flowers.

Suddenly they came out of the flowers into a strip of grass and found a small canal in front of them.

"Oh, shucks!" Mandie exclaimed. "How are we going to get across that water?"

"I don't think we have time to figure that out tonight," Jonathan said as he stared at the blades of the windmill that stood just across the canal from them.

"Yes, we'd better wait till tomorrow in the daylight to find a way over," Celia agreed.

"I don't see any lights in the miller's cottage. He must be gone to bed," Mandie said.

Jonathan grinned at her as he replied, "I imagine everyone is in bed at this time of night except us three 'reckless people.' "

"Jonathan, you're making fun of me," Mandie said, with a smirk.

"No, I'm not. I'm just using the word you used to describe yourself to your grandmother," he told her.

Mandie quickly changed the subject. "Let's look for a way across the canal." She walked along the edge of the water.

"There is no way in sight, Mandie," Jonathan said. "And I don't think we'd better go wandering around in the dark."

Mandie stomped her foot impatiently. "Then let's just go back to the house."

"That's exactly what we should do. Come on," Jonathan said, turning to walk back down the lane they had come.

Mandie reluctantly followed him, and Celia stayed by her side. Mandie kept looking back at the blades of the windmill. If Jonathan was right about such things, why were the blades in the wrong position? Were they set to give some special message from the miller? Or had they accidentally slipped?

Jonathan suddenly stopped in front of the girls, causing them to bump into him.

"I just had an idea. Maybe the blades are set for some kind of distress signal," he said excitedly, looking back at the windmill in the distance.

"I was thinking the same thing," Mandie said, catching her balance as Celia straightened up beside her. "I wish we could go over there and talk to that miller."

Jonathan turned to walk on. "Not tonight, Mandie," he said.

The girls followed him, and Mandie stopped and turned for a last glimpse of the windmill.

Suddenly the blades changed position. She screamed excitedly, "Look! The blades are moving!" She began to run back toward the canal.

Jonathan and Celia caught up with her and stood at the edge of the water, watching as the blades swung round and round and finally came to a stop.

"They're in the right place now," Jonathan told the girls. "See, they're at one-thirty, four-thirty, seven-thirty, and ten-thirty, which is where they should be for the night."

"I wonder who did that," Mandie said, trying to squint through the darkness. "I can't see anyone over there."

"It's too far. Besides, the mechanism is probably controlled inside the base of the windmill," Jonathan told her.

"I'm so anxious to get over there and see everything," Mandie said.

"We'd better go back to the house now, Mandie," Celia urged her.

"I suppose so," Mandie agreed with a sigh.

As they turned to walk back the way they had come, Mandie suddenly saw someone move among the tall, flowering bushes nearby. She held out her hands to stop her friends.

"Shhh!" she whispered. "There's someone over there." She pointed to their left.

Jonathan and Celia looked in that direction. Then Jonathan whispered hoarsely, "Let's see who it is!" He made a quick rush in the direction of the moving bushes.

A figure jumped up and ran. The three young people

quickly followed, pushing their way through the field of flowers. Whoever it was seemed to have longer legs than theirs, and they couldn't catch up.

Suddenly Mandie's long skirt became tangled in something, hindering her movement. She reached down in the darkness to shake it free and found her hand in the briars of a rosebush.

"Oh, I'm all tangled up in thorns!" she exclaimed, putting the fingers that had been stuck into her mouth.

"Just hold still," Jonathan told her. He found a stick nearby and came to push the stems of the roses away from her skirt. "Go slowly. When I hold one back, make a little step forward, one at a time."

Mandie did as she was told. Celia managed to grasp the top of some stems where there weren't any thorns, and held them away from Mandie. Finally she was free. As she shook out her skirts, she quickly looked into the distance. The figure had completely disappeared. They had no way now of knowing who it was.

"I guess I caused us to lose whoever it was," she told her friends.

"Either of us could have gotten tangled in the rose-bushes," Jonathan said.

"Well, let's go back to the house," Mandie said in a disappointed tone.

As they walked back, they were careful to stay on the lanes and out of the flowers. This time the crooked pathway they had chosen led by the barn. It was a huge structure, almost as large as the house. They stopped to have a look.

Mandie started to speak, but was suddenly aware of someone sitting on a stool nearby. She grasped her friends' hands and pointed. The three of them edged closer, and then they all realized it was Dieter.

Mandie tried to slip by him, but the rustle of her skirts in the bushes caused the man to look up from the pipe he was filling with tobacco. He immediately stood up and smiled at the three young people.

Remembering that he could hear but not speak, Mandie advanced closer and said cordially, "Good evening, Mr. Dieter."

His smile grew wider, and he bowed slightly as the three moved on by. The pathway led around the house and up to the front door. Mandie walked ahead to open it.

"Don't forget to be real quiet," she whispered as she tried the door handle, but it wouldn't turn. "It's locked!" she gasped.

"Let me try," Jonathan offered, but he couldn't budge it either.

"Let's go around to the back door," Celia suggested.

The three quietly walked around the house. Jonathan stepped up to the back door and tried it. It was also locked.

"Now, what are we going to do?" Celia asked.

"I don't know, but we've got to do something. We can't stay out here all night," Mandie said as she looked around the stoop.

"I'll try a window," Jonathan suggested, and the three looked for one that would be easy to get to. The house was built low to the ground and the entire ground floor seemed to be accessible.

"How about that one?" Jonathan whispered as he pushed through flower bushes to reach a window at the right of the door.

The girls watched as he tried opening it. But the window was securely locked. They went to every window they could reach and were not able to open any of them.

Stepping back, Mandie looked at the story above. "Do you think we could reach any of those windows?"

"Mandie, I'm sure we left the window open in our room," Celia said.

"That's right. Let's go around that end and see if we can climb up to it," Mandie said.

They hurried to the corner of the house and looked up at the windows to their room. There was one window open, but it looked like a long, straight climb to get to it.

"How can we get up there?" Mandie asked.

"Why don't we just go back and ask Dieter to let us in?" Jonathan suggested.

"Well, I suppose we could," Mandie reluctantly agreed. "You go get him, and Celia and I will wait right here."

Jonathan hurried back toward the barn. The girls kept looking at the windows above.

Soon Mandie began to wonder where Jonathan had gone. He'd had plenty of time to go to the barn and back, but there was no sign of him. He couldn't have gotten lost.

"Maybe we ought to go see where Jonathan went," Mandie whispered to Celia.

"Maybe," Celia agreed.

Suddenly there was a low hissing sound, and the girls looked up to see Jonathan standing on the roof with a coiled rope in his hands.

"I'm going to tie this to the chimney and throw it down to you," he whispered hoarsely.

The girls nodded.

"Why don't you just go in the window of our room and come down and unlock the door?" Mandie whispered back.

Jonathan silently agreed. They watched as he secured

the rope around the chimney, and then grasping it tightly he swung down and dangled in front of the window to the girls' room. Finally he caught a toehold and slid through over the windowsill. Then he leaned back out the window and waved to the girls.

Mandie and Celia hastened around the house to the front door to wait for him. Just as they stepped on the stoop, the door swung wide and Anna came out of the house. She stopped in surprise at seeing the girls, and then went on down the pathway.

"At least she left the door open for us," Mandie said with relief as she and Celia stepped inside and Jonathan appeared at the foot of the stairs. "Anna opened the door and came out," Mandie told Jonathan.

"Good," Jonathan said with a big breath. "I couldn't find Dieter."

"Let's all go to our rooms," Celia said, tiptoeing up the stairway.

Mandie and Jonathan quickly followed her up the stairs and down the hallway. Jonathan waved good-night as he went to the end where his room was. Mandie and Celia came to their room and found the door standing wide open.

"Snowball! Jonathan must have left the door open!" Mandie said excitedly, rushing into their room and then to the bathroom. "Snowball's gone!"

"Oh, Mandie, what are we going to do?" Celia asked as they stood there in the middle of the room.

"We're going to have to find him before we can go to bed," Mandie told her.

"I hope he didn't get out of the house," Celia said.

"Come on, let's get Jonathan to help. We've got to find him," Mandie said as she went out into the hallway and on toward Jonathan's room. Celia followed.

Because they had just arrived that day, they weren't familiar with the house. They had no idea where the servants stayed, or the layout of the rest of the house. But they would soon know every nook and cranny, because Snowball had to be found.

Chapter 4 / Where Had Snowball Been?

"Jonathan!" Mandie whispered outside his door as she knocked softly.

He immediately opened the door and asked, "What's wrong?"

"You left our door open and Snowball got out and is gone. Will you help us look for him?" Mandie asked.

"I didn't leave your door open. It was standing open when I went through your window. I'm sorry Snowball has escaped. But don't worry, I'll help you find him," the boy told her as he joined the girls in the hallway.

"How are we going to do this?" Celia asked.

"We don't know this house at all, so this is going to be difficult," Mandie answered.

Jonathan thought for a moment and said, "We certainly can't look in the rooms that are occupied by your grandmother or the senator's room, but I suppose the rest are vacant."

"But, Jonathan, where do you think the servants stay?

We don't want to disturb them," Mandie said.

"You said Anna went out when you came in, and we saw Dieter at the barn, so maybe they have rooms in the barn where William is staying," Jonathan said.

"All right, but what about Gretchen?" Mandie asked.

"I don't know, but I'd say it's probably clear, except for your grandmother and Senator Morton," Jonathan replied. "Let's start with our rooms."

They hurried down the hall to check the girls' room thoroughly, in case Snowball was hiding in there somewhere. "He's not here!" Mandie declared as she knelt down and looked under the big bed.

"Or here," Jonathan said, searching the bathroom.

Celia went through the wardrobe. "He's not here either."

"Your room next, Jonathan," Mandie decided. "Let's take this small lamp with us." She picked up the lighted oil lamp from a table. "I hope it doesn't go out."

The boy's room was similar to the girls', and after a careful search Snowball wasn't found there either. They began opening doors to the other rooms along the corridor, searching each one.

As they checked the last room, Mandie said, "You know, Snowball couldn't be in any of these rooms, because all the doors are shut!" She was still carrying the lamp.

"Unless someone opened a door and he slipped inside the room," Jonathan suggested.

"Now what? Shall we go downstairs?" Celia asked.

"I suppose so. That's all that's left except the attic— if this house has one," Mandie said. Holding the lamp high to see, she led the way toward the staircase.

On the ground floor they found sitting rooms, the parlor, the dining room, the kitchen, a large pantry room, the storeroom, a sewing room, various closets, and a large glassed-in room full of growing plants and flowers.

The moonlight came through the glass skylights and windows and they didn't really need the lamp to see, but Mandie held on to it. She sniffed the air. "There are roses growing in here. I can smell them."

"And there are some yellow flowers here that have a nice scent, too," Celia said as she bent toward the blossoms.

"How about these purple ones?" Jonathan asked. "I don't know what they are. They don't have any smell, and they feel rough."

"I don't know, but they're all so beautiful," Mandie declared. "I suppose Dieter takes care of all this." She walked around looking at the many varieties of flowers.

"Mandie, don't you think we ought to look for Snowball and get back to our rooms?" Celia asked.

"You're right, Celia. It is late," Mandie agreed as she began looking under tables and behind boxes, calling the kitten's name. "He's not here. Well, that leaves the attic, unless there is a cellar in this house."

Jonathan had already found what must be the door to the cellar. It was securely locked. "He couldn't be in the cellar. It's locked," he said.

"Let's see if there's an attic, then," Mandie said, turning to leave the room. She noticed a door behind some tall plants that she had not seen before in the semi-darkness. "Here's one more door," she said, going over to it. As she reached it, the lamp went out.

Jonathan and Celia joined Mandie as she turned the latch and the door swung open by itself. They stood there trying to see into the dark room.

"I can't see a thing," Mandie said, putting her hands in front of her as she slowly stepped inside. There was only a glint of moonlight in the room.

Celia and Jonathan followed close behind. "It must be a storeroom," Jonathan whispered.

At that moment they heard someone clear their throat. The three froze in their tracks, waiting to see what would happen next. As her eyes became more accustomed to the darkness, Mandie could see a faint outline of a bed in the far corner. Then suddenly someone sat up on the bed. Mandie thought it looked like Anna, and she backed out of the room, pushing Celia and Jonathan behind her. She touched the door and it closed behind them.

The three hurried across the flower room and went back through the door to the hallway where they had entered. Then they paused for a breath in the dim moonlight.

"Do y'all think that was Anna?" Mandie asked in a whisper.

"It looked like her," Celia said.

"It could have been," Jonathan agreed.

"That sure is a strange place to have a bedroom—behind the flower room," Mandie remarked.

"Yes, but what about Snowball?" Jonathan asked.

"Oh, Snowball is so much trouble sometimes!" Mandie exclaimed. "I just wonder who let him out of our room."

"Gretchen knew you had brought him here; so did Dieter, because he made the sandbox . . ." Celia began.

"And William also knew, but he is supposed to be staying in the barn," Mandie said. "I'm sure Anna saw me holding him when we first came in today and tried to talk to her."

"It was probably an accident—leaving the door open,

I mean. Someone just wasn't used to having a cat in the house," Jonathan said.

"But what was anyone doing in our room?" Mandie asked.

Jonathan shrugged his shoulders and said, "Who knows? Maybe Gretchen went in for some reason."

"But, Jonathan, think how late it is. It was already bedtime when we went out," Mandie said. "What would Gretchen, or anyone else for that matter, be doing in our room at that hour?"

"I don't know, but are we going to try to find the attic?" Jonathan asked.

"That's all that's left." Mandie ascended the stairs to the second floor. Celia and Jonathan followed.

They paused at the top of the steps. "We need another lamp," Mandie said. "Jonathan, have you got an extra one in your room?"

"I think so," he said. "I'll see."

The three quietly walked down the corridor to Jonathan's room, and the girls waited while he went inside and then returned with a small oil lamp, brightly burning.

"This one has plenty of oil," Jonathan said, holding it up for the girls to see the supply of oil splashing around in the glass base.

"When we searched all the rooms on this floor, I don't remember seeing a door to an attic, or anything that looked like one," Mandie said as they stood there.

"Neither do I," Celia said.

"I didn't either, but if there's an attic there's got to be a door, and from the looks of the house outside I'd say there's an attic," Jonathan declared.

"Well, let's begin right here," Mandie said, opening the door to the first room they came to.

All the doors led into rooms. "I suppose we'll have to

look in each room again to see if there's a door inside that leads to an attic," Mandie decided.

They looked in every room, and finally in the last one, a small bedroom, they found another door.

"This must be it," Mandie said, and pushing at it, she added, "And of course it's locked."

"We have been over every inch of this house, Mandie, except the locked doors. Snowball just isn't in the house," Jonathan declared.

Mandie sighed deeply, fidgeted with her long, blonde braid, and said, "I sure hope he hasn't gone outside and gotten lost."

"I'll go with you and look around the yard," Jonathan offered.

"All right. Celia, you stay inside so we don't get locked out this time," Mandie told her friend.

"Please don't be too long, Mandie. We're going to have to go to bed sometime tonight," Celia reminded her.

Mandie smiled and said, "We'll be right back. Don't get scared now. Nothing's going to bother you. You'll be safe inside the house. Just watch for us and be sure we can get back in."

Celia looked at her and said, "Mandie, I'm not afraid. I'll wait for y'all. I hope you find Snowball."

Mandie and Jonathan circled the house as they looked through all the shrubbery and flowering bushes. Now and then Mandie softly called to Snowball, "Snowball, where are you? Come here. Kitty, kitty, kitty."

They even went as far as the barn, but they didn't go inside for fear of waking William and whoever else was sleeping there. Snowball just didn't seem to be anywhere.

"Well, I guess we have to go back and go to bed," Mandie admitted after one last look around the barn. "I just wonder how he got out."

"Maybe he'll come back on his own. You said he had done that before," Jonathan told her as they walked back to the house, still watching for the white kitten.

"This is a strange place to him and I'm not sure he could find the way back," Mandie said. "I'll get up as soon as it's light in the morning and look for him again."

Celia was waiting and opened the door for them. She glanced at Mandie and said, "No Snowball?"

"No Snowball," Mandie told her. "Let's go to bed."

The three young people went back to their rooms for the night. Jonathan promised to help the girls look for the missing cat in the morning.

Mandie and Celia talked for a little while after they went to bed, but Celia fell asleep. Mandie tossed and turned, wondering where her precious white kitten was. He was her link to her father's home. Shortly after her father had died her stepmother remarried, and Mandie was farmed out to another family in Swain County. She worked as a baby-sitter and was overloaded with other responsibilities.

As she lay there thinking, Mandie remembered snatching up Snowball in her father's yard and taking him with her. He was the only thing left from her father's home. Of course she still had Uncle Ned, her father's old Cherokee friend, but Snowball was all hers. She could see her father watching her feed the scrawny little kitten when he was born. Snowball's mother had disappeared before Snowball was old enough to eat by himself, and Jim Shaw had taught Mandie how to give the tiny kitten a drop of milk at a time with an eyedropper.

Tears filled Mandie's eyes and she whispered a word to God: "Please, dear God, send my kitten back to me. Please."

She finally fell asleep and dreamed. She was back

home at Charley Gap, and her father was building the fence around his property. Snowball was chasing butterflies through the tall grass.

Suddenly something hit Mandie hard in the stomach as she slept. She felt it in her dream but didn't wake up.

Celia woke first the next morning. She rubbed her eyes and sat up, remembering that Mandie wanted to look for Snowball as soon as it was daylight.

A movement on the bed caught her attention. She gasped. There was Snowball—turning round and round, as he did sometimes when he couldn't decide which way to lie down. *Where did he come from?*

Celia quickly shook Mandie. "Look, Mandie! Snowball's back!"

Mandie was wide awake at once, and sat up to find her white kitten curled up next to her.

"Snowball! How did you get back? Where have you been?" she asked all at once, picking him up and smoothing his white fur. Tears of joy filled her blue eyes.

Celia was excited and happy for her friend. "He found his way back somehow, didn't he?"

"Thank goodness," Mandie replied. "We'd better let Jonathan know."

The girls jumped out of bed and quickly dressed, then hurried down the hallway to Jonathan's room where they tapped lightly on his door. Mandie held Snowball securely, even though she had put his leash on him.

Jonathan came to the door immediately. He was already fully dressed. "Where did you find him?"

"We didn't find him. He found us. When we woke up this morning he was on our bed!" Mandie explained.

"Well, you silly cat, causing all that trouble and then calmly showing up on your own," Jonathan said, ruffling the fur on Snowball's head.

Snowball didn't like the fur on his head ruffled, and he batted at Jonathan with his paw.

"I'm just glad he's all right," Mandie said.

"Me too. Let's go downstairs and see if breakfast is ready. It's almost time," Jonathan reminded the girls.

The three hurried down to the dining room and found Gretchen setting the table.

"Good morning, Gretchen. Do you mind if we sit down and wait?" Mandie asked the girl.

"That you may do," Gretchen said with a smile and a wave toward some chairs. "I will bring the coffee while we wait for madam and the gentleman."

She left the room, and the young people sat down at the table. Mandie tied Snowball's leash to the table leg.

"Grandmother and Senator Morton should be along soon. We're going to Delfshaven Port, remember?" Mandie remarked with a yawn. "And I do hope Grandmother will take us to see the windmill. I want to go all the way across the canal."

"We forgot to look out our window this morning to see where the blades were stopped on the windmill," Celia told her.

"Some detectives you girls make," Jonathan teased.

"With all the excitement we've had, I don't believe you would have remembered to look out at the windmill this morning, either," Mandie answered.

Jonathan's face sobered. "No, I don't suppose I would have. And I'm glad your cat came back from wherever he was."

"I'd like to know who left our door open and let him out," Mandie said. "And I'd like to find out who it was that saw us in the dark and then ran when we went to look at the windmill."

"Maybe we'll be able to solve these mysteries," Jonathan said. "And we should also find out who set the blades on the windmill at an odd position, and then moved them back to normal. Uncle Ned was right. There are mysteries here in Holland, too."

"Well, he couldn't have known about all this," Mandie said.

"I've come to the conclusion that he never knows too much about any mystery in particular," Jonathan said. "He just knows you will find one wherever you go."

Celia smiled. "Mandie is always chasing unexplained happenings."

Before Mandie could defend herself, Gretchen brought the tray, set it down, and poured their cups full of steaming fresh coffee. Mandie breathed deeply to inhale the delicious smell.

"As soon as madam and the gentleman arrive, I will bring the food," Gretchen said with a smile. Then she left the room.

In fact, she met Mrs. Taft and Senator Morton at the door.

After exchanging morning greetings, they sat down with the young people, and Gretchen returned shortly to serve their breakfast. Then, without comment, she took Snowball to the kitchen to feed him.

"Did y'all sleep well?" Mrs. Taft asked as she buttered a fresh roll.

"Yes, ma'am," Celia and Jonathan answered as they sipped the hot coffee.

"I dreamed of my father," Mandie said with a sad expression on her face. "I was back at Charley Gap with him and Snowball."

"Snowball!" Mrs. Taft spoke as if the kitten's name brought something to mind. "Amanda, you're going to have to do something about that cat."

"What do you mean, Grandmother?" Mandie asked, her heart pounding at Mrs. Taft's stern voice.

"I'll tell you what. Sometime in the middle of the night that cat jumped onto my bed and almost scared me out of my wits. I was sound asleep, and to be awakened like that was very unsettling," Mrs. Taft explained.

The three young people quickly looked at one another, and Mandie recalled the thump on her stomach in her dream.

"Grandmother, did you put Snowball back in our room?" Mandie asked anxiously, leaning forward.

"Yes, I did. When I put him on the floor he jumped right up on your bed," Mrs. Taft said. "I was surprised he didn't wake you. How did he get out, Amanda?" She waited impatiently for an answer.

"I—I—don't know," Mandie began, twisting the napkin in her lap. "Someone left our door open, and we had to search the house for him—"

"When did someone leave your door open, Amanda? You had Snowball with you when we went on our walk after supper, and when we returned for the night," Mrs. Taft said.

"I know, Grandmother," Mandie replied, then quickly added, "We went back outside to look at the windmill, and left him in the room. When we came back he was gone and the door was standing open—"

"You all went back outside after we said good-night?" Mrs. Taft asked in disbelief.

"Yes, ma'am," Celia answered for Mandie.

"We only went to look at the windmill," Jonathan offered.

"And we came right back," Mandie added rapidly. "It isn't far. You can see the windmill from our window."

"At that time of night you could have gotten lost,"

Mrs. Taft said firmly. "This is a strange place to all of us, and I will not allow the three of you to be running around after dark. Is that understood?"

"Yes, ma'am," Celia replied.

"I understand, Grandmother, and I'm sorry," Mandie said.

"I apologize, too, Mrs. Taft," Jonathan added.

"Now finish your breakfast. We've got some sightseeing to do," Mrs. Taft said briskly, draining her coffee cup.

"Is it all right if I take Snowball with us, Grandmother?" Mandie asked, cleaning up her plate.

"I suppose," Mrs. Taft consented. "I don't know what else we can do with him but leave him in your room. And then there's the chance that someone may let him out again. But you've absolutely got to hold on to him, Amanda. I will not have him interfering with our pleasure."

As they all stood to leave, Gretchen stuck her head in the door with Snowball on his leash.

"He acts up very much," Gretchen told Mandie. "He has a big taste for food."

The three young people laughed at the maid's appraisal of Snowball.

Mandie took the cat in her arms and wrapped the leash around her wrist. "Oh, he'd eat all the time if you gave him the food. Thanks, Gretchen."

Mrs. Taft and Senator Morton led the way outside to the carriage where William was waiting for them. The young people lagged behind to keep their conversation out of earshot.

"Whew, that was close!" Jonathan blew out his breath, making the dark curls on his forehead fly.

"Yes, but we still don't know who let Snowball out, or who it was that we saw in the field last night," Mandie remarked as they waited for her grandmother and the senator to enter the vehicle. "Or who changed the wind-mill blades."

"Mandie, we barely managed to get by with leaving the house after dark," Celia reminded her in a low whisper. "I sure hope you don't intend to pursue any of those questions further."

"Maybe we won't have to pursue anything. Maybe it'll all come to us," Mandie said with a smile as she stepped into the carriage.

Chapter 5 / Albert Appears

The countryside was in full bloom. Brightly colored flowers filled the air with many scents as a soft breeze swayed their petals. The golden sunshine glistened on the waters of the canals. Now and then a bird call could be heard above the scrunching of the carriage wheels in the loose pebbles of the road, and the clopping of the horses.

"Oh, it's all so perfect," Mandie exclaimed as she leaned on the window. "So beautiful and so refreshing! It makes me want to get out and walk."

"I'd rather just sit here and float through it all," Celia said with a little laugh as she gazed outside.

"And just think, my ancestors left all this for New York," Jonathan remarked. He quickly turned to Mandie and added, "According to your grandmother, your ancestors left here for the United States. You know, we could have some mutual relatives way back in history."

Mandie quickly told him, "But you are from the North

58

and we're from the South. My ancestors may never have traveled north for all we know. Anyway, my Cherokee ancestors were already in the southern part of the country before the white man ever came to the United States."

"What about before that, Mandie? Where did the Cherokees come from?" Celia asked.

Mandie was at a loss. She had never thought about that. "I really don't know," she said slowly. "But I'll ask Uncle Ned when we see him. He'll know."

"But he's not your real uncle," Jonathan said. "He was just your father's friend."

"Yes, but he's full-blooded Cherokee. Therefore all his ancestors were there before the white people came," Mandie said. "And speaking of Uncle Ned, I do hope he shows up sometime soon. He might be able to help us solve some of the mysteries we've run into." She quickly glanced at her grandmother to see if she had heard, but she was deep in conversation with Senator Morton.

"Oh, Mandie, we haven't run into any real big mysteries here," Jonathan remarked. "At least not like the ones we came across in some of the other countries we visited."

"That's because they haven't been fully developed yet," Mandie assured him. "Give it some time, and we'll have an intriguing adventure on our hands with the mystery of the windmill blades. Just wait and see." Her blue eyes sparkled with excitement as she thought about the possibility of becoming involved in the solution to the puzzle.

Mandie was anxious to visit the miller and ask about the position of the blades the night before. Her grandmother had insisted they go see the port today, but maybe there would still be time left for the windmill. Mandie thought the house help was kind of mysterious too.

With Anna deaf and Dieter not able to say a word, that left Gretchen to talk for everyone. And she didn't seem to be very interested in anything except her duties as a maid. There was William, their driver, but he was not from the area, so he wouldn't know anything about the windmill.

"I don't see how we'll ever find out who set the windmill blades to that unusual position," Celia said, looking puzzled. She glanced out the window then, and said, "Looks like we're coming into a village."

Mrs. Taft explained, "This is the little port town. Most of these buildings and houses are very, very old. Some of them were probably built before our ancestors sailed for America."

Mandie and her friends watched, intrigued, as they passed quaint structures built low to the ground. The people walking along the way were dressed in native Dutch costume. The women and girls wore full skirts with laced bodices, and headpieces with wide brims that turned back, leaving the pointed ends floppy. The men and boys were dressed in full, gathered pants and bloused shirts. Everyone wore wooden shoes.

"Look at their shoes!" Mandie exclaimed as she gazed at the people's feet. "I've just got to buy a pair of wooden shoes to take home!"

"Me too," Celia echoed.

"I can assure you they are not comfortable to wear," Jonathan told them. "I tried a pair when I went to school here."

"I don't care, I like them," Mandie said. "I wonder how they are made?"

"They take a block of wood, usually willow, and carve the shoe from that," Jonathan explained. "What I'd really like to have is one of their windmills in my backyard."

"A windmill?" Mandie frowned at the boy. "It would be impossible to take one of those home."

Mrs. Taft, having heard her remark, spoke to Mandie: "No, dear, not entirely impossible. Even stone buildings can be moved from country to country. They dismantle it, stone by stone, and then reconstruct it at the new location."

Mandie turned to Jonathan. "Well, in that case, tell your father to buy you a windmill. He can afford it."

Jonathan smiled at her and said, "You don't know my father. He may have the money, but he's awfully particular as to how he spends it. Besides, I'm always gone away to a school somewhere, and my father is always traveling on business, so why buy a windmill?"

"I'm sorry your mother is not living, Jonathan, so you could stay home in New York instead of being educated all over the world," Mandie consoled. Then with a laugh she added, "But then we never would have met you and had the benefit of your knowledge in our travels here in Europe."

Senator Morton was listening to the conversation, and he told Jonathan, "I'll check just as soon as we get back to the house to see if your father has sent a wire telling us when he'll join us."

"Thank you, sir," Jonathan said. He paused and then added, "What I'd really like to do is spend some time with my aunt and uncle in Paris. I haven't seen them in a long time."

"Perhaps they will have sent us a message before we leave Holland, as to when they'll be back home in Paris," Senator Morton said with a smile.

"Please don't worry about it, sir," Jonathan said. "I'm really and truly enjoying traveling with you people."

The driver was bringing the carriage to a halt near a

wharf. Mrs. Taft told the young people, "We'll be getting out for a walk about the port."

Holding Snowball in her arms, Mandie quickly looked around as they stepped out of the carriage. The town seemed small, but the harbor was full of ships with various flags. Evidently the place was a busy, thriving seaport. Her grandmother had told them Delftshaven Port was part of Rotterdam, but that they would not explore anything other than the port for lack of time.

"Come along, Amanda," Mrs. Taft said, reaching for Mandie's hand. "Let's walk along the wharf here, so when you get back home you can say you walked where your ancestors walked before leaving for America. Someday I'll take you to Plymouth Rock, where they landed."

Senator Morton joined Mrs. Taft on the other side, assisting her over the rough surface before they stepped onto the planked wharf. Jonathan and Celia followed close behind.

Mandie noticed several sailors loading and unloading the ships. A mixture of sounds filled the air—the sailors calling to one another, their laughter, some singing somewhere out of sight, and the noise of the freight itself being handled.

Snowball squirmed to be free. Mandie let him down to walk, but held firmly to his leash. "I think he smells fish," she told her friends.

"Better hold on to him tightly," Jonathan warned her.

Mrs. Taft glanced sharply at the kitten. "Amanda, whatever you do, do not let that cat get loose."

Mandie tightened her grip on the leash. "I won't, Grandmother. He just wants some exercise."

"Let's go sit for a few minutes, over there on that wall," Mrs. Taft said. She and Senator Morton led the way to a low, rough seawall, a safe distance from the scurrying workmen.

The young people followed and sat near the adults, Mandie all the while securing Snowball's leash as tightly as possible.

"Let's spend a few moments of silence in memory of our ancestors who were brave enough to sail the seas in such uncivilized days," Mrs. Taft said somberly, staring out across the water, "and who allowed us the privilege of being born in the United States."

Mandie didn't feel any connection just now with this country, or her ancestors who left Holland for America. All she could think of was the mystery of the windmill blades, and the person from the parade who ran from them in the dark. She couldn't think of any reason why he should avoid them. And she was sure he was the same person who had left the parade with the blonde girl. Her memory for faces always rang true. *Did he live near the house where they were staying?* she wondered. *What was he doing in the flower field?*

In her reverie, Mandie had loosened her hold on Snowball's leash. She felt a tug, but managed to hold on to it as her kitten bristled at something on the ground. Leaning forward, Mandie saw a mouse sitting right beside her grandmother's long skirt.

Trying not to startle Mrs. Taft, Mandie gently touched her arm and spoke in a low voice, "Don't move, Grandmother. Snowball has found a mouse."

Mrs. Taft grabbed her long skirts and jumped up from her seat on the wall. The mouse ran in circles and then headed straight for Mrs. Taft's shoes. Snowball made a quick lunge and caught the rodent in his teeth, shaking it and then letting it go.

"Thank goodness that cat was with us!" Mrs. Taft exclaimed. She sat down again and fanned her face with a lace handkerchief.

The senator seemed at a loss for words. Finally he said, "It's gone now. When the cat let it go, it ran off."

"I'm glad he let it go," Mandie said. "I wouldn't want him smelling like a mouse." She made a face. "You're a pretty smart kitty, Snowball."

"Remember the mouse in our room back at school?" Celia reminded Mandie. "We were both scared to death, almost."

"Yes, I remember—"

"Amanda, Jonathan, Celia, I think we'd better be going," Mrs. Taft addressed the young people as she stood.

"Yes, Grandmother," Mandie replied as she picked up Snowball. *Thank goodness, this ancestor business is being cut short. Maybe there will still be time to go to the miller's house,* Mandie thought.

"We must look for some place to eat," Mrs. Taft said.

"Yes. I haven't seen anything close by, have you?" Senator Morton asked as he helped her into the carriage.

William, the driver, stood by holding the door. "If I may be so forward, sir, I know of a small inn on the other side of the village. It is nice and clean, and well-patronized by travelers such as yourselves."

"Thank you, William," Senator Morton said. Then he turned to Mrs. Taft. "Shall we try the inn that William suggests?"

"Yes, that would be fine. It's getting late for the noon meal, and I'm sure everyone is hungry."

"Take us there, William," Senator Morton told the driver.

The young people couldn't conceal their delight that food was next on the agenda.

William drove through the village and out onto a country road. Shortly, they came within sight of a picturesque white inn standing in a field of beautiful flowers.

Willow trees cast lacy patterns on the outside walls.

Mandie eagerly watched as they approached the structure. There were several other horses and carriages in the pebble-covered yard. William pulled their vehicle up alongside one and jumped down to open the door.

"William was right," Jonathan observed. "These carriages reveal the status of the patrons here."

"And aren't the horses absolutely beautiful!" Celia exclaimed.

"Well, Jonathan, you are the expert on carriages and wealth," Mandie said, "and Celia, you know all about horses. But I'll tell you what kind of people own them after we get inside."

William stepped ahead to open the inn door for Mrs. Taft and Senator Morton. A man in Dutch costume greeted them. The young people stared at the rich interior as they stepped inside. It was like a room out of a palace. Blue velvet draperies hung at the floor-length windows. The tables were covered with white linen and elegantly set with crystal and china. A small group of musicians played soft music at the far end of the room.

"It's breathtaking!" Mandie exclaimed.

"Of course," Jonathan acknowledged. "William said it was patronized by travelers such as Mrs. Taft and the senator. Meaning, of course, the wealthy. The owner collects big prices and can afford this kind of a place."

As the head waiter led them to a table, Mandie observed the faces of the diners already seated. An older man and woman at a table nearby seemed to be in a heated argument in a language that Mandie couldn't understand.

She sat down between Celia and Jonathan and whispered, "What language are those people speaking?"

Jonathan whispered back, "Don't tell me you've already forgotten the sound of Italian. We were just in Italy a short while ago."

"Oh, Jonathan, I've been through so many countries and languages, they're all jumbled up in my head. What are they talking about?"

"They can't agree on what to take back home with them for their daughter who is evidently engaged to be married."

"There is a nice-looking man at the table in front of us who keeps staring at us," Mandie whispered to her friends without looking at him.

Celia and Jonathan looked at the young man and he smiled at them. Then he waved slightly at Mandie. Mandie felt her face turn red.

"Jonathan, Celia, why did y'all look at him? Now he knows we're talking about him," Mandie said, her head bent so the man couldn't see her face.

"He's alone. Maybe he'd like to speak to someone. I know how that is from traveling around the world in so many schools—always alone and no one to talk to," Jonathan said.

"Amanda, Celia, Jonathan, please listen to what the man is saying," Mrs. Taft spoke across the table.

The three looked up to see that she meant the waiter, who stood waiting to take their orders.

"Now, would you please recite one more time the food that is being served?" Mrs. Taft asked the waiter.

Mandie continued to feel uncomfortable about the man at the next table, who was still looking their way. The waiter spoke rapidly and with a sharp accent, so that Mandie didn't understand a thing he said until he said "ham."

"Ham—that's what I'll have, please," Mandie said quickly. At least ham sounded familiar, although she had

learned that the names of foods back home weren't nec-
essarily the same thing in foreign countries.

"I will have the same," Celia said.

"And add me, please," Jonathan told the waiter.

Mrs. Taft and the senator had already ordered, and
the waiter left the table.

Mandie asked her grandmother, "Where are we going
next?"

"I wanted to go to Delft to see the Delftware factory,
but I'd like to have plenty of time when we go there, so
maybe we'll save that for tomorrow," Mrs. Taft replied.

"We could go for a boat ride on a canal this afternoon," Senator Morton suggested.

"Or we could go see the windmill near the house
where we're staying," Mandie said quickly, smiling at her
grandmother.

"Dear, we don't know the miller, and one doesn't just
go popping in on strangers. The miller lives there, you
know," her grandmother explained. "And we'd have to
get his permission to see the windmill. We'll have to wait
until that can all be arranged."

"Oh, shucks!" Mandie said with resignation. "So now
what?"

"William mentioned that there is to be a flower parade
in a village west of here this afternoon. Maybe that would
be interesting, since we weren't able to see the whole
parade we happened onto yesterday," Mrs. Taft said. "Unless, of course, you'd all like to take a boat ride on the
canal, as the senator suggests."

Another flower parade! Mandie thought quickly.
*Maybe the girl and young man we saw leave the other
parade would be in this one too.*

"What do you think?" Mandie asked Celia and Jonathan, hoping they'd prefer the parade.

"I'd enjoy the parade, Mrs. Taft," Celia said.

"Do the same people take part in all the parades?" Jonathan asked. "I suppose you couldn't possibly know that. Anyway, I'd like to see it, if that's agreeable to everyone."

Mrs. Taft looked to the senator. He smiled and nodded, and she added, "Then as soon as we finish eating here, we'll get William to find the place for us."

The waiter brought the steaming plates of food. Mandie found the ham to be delicious, but with a slightly sweeter taste than the ham back home. She put some scraps in a saucer and placed it under the table for Snowball, whose leash was tied to the table leg. As she raised up, she caught the young man at the next table looking at her again. She quickly looked away.

"I wish that man—" Mandie began to whisper to her friends. Then she saw him get up and approach her grandmother. She stopped with her mouth open and listened.

The man bent over slightly to speak to Mrs. Taft. He was tall and blond, with twinkling blue eyes.

"Madam, please forgive this intrusion, but I believe we are neighbors, temporary though it may be," he began. Mrs. Taft looked up at him. "My name is Albert Van Dongen. My father owns the flour mill near where you are staying."

"Flour mill?" Mrs. Taft questioned.

"Yes, madam, the one with the windmill that you can see from your house," the young man went on.

"The windmill!" Mandie gasped.

"I'm sorry, I haven't introduced myself and the others—" Mrs. Taft began.

"That is not necessary, Madam Taft, Senator Morton," Albert said. "You see, we have servants who carry the news of visitors in the area."

Senator Morton stood up to shake hands with the young man. "I believe we've had some discussion about your father's windmill," he said, winking at Mandie and her friends.

"It is just an ordinary windmill, sir. It operates the flour mill," Albert explained.

"Could we see it, please?" Mandie asked anxiously.

Albert smiled at her and said, "Of course, miss, anytime you wish."

"Oh, thank you!" Mandie replied, beaming brightly.

"Yes, I'm afraid the young people have been anxious to see your father's windmill up close," Mrs. Taft explained. "You see, we don't have such things back in the United States, where we come from."

"I have been at the port to take care of some shipments for my father, but I am ready to return home now. Perhaps you would like to come with me," Albert said to Mrs. Taft.

The three young people held their breath awaiting her reply. Mrs. Taft glanced at them and then asked the senator, "Do you think we should?"

"Of course, why not? The offer is too good to be turned down," Senator Morton said.

Mandie smiled broadly.

"All right then, Mr. Van Dongen, we will be happy to accept your invitation, provided you think it will be all right with your father," Mrs. Taft said.

"Of course it will be all right with my father," Albert assured her. "He enjoys showing off his windmill anytime." He turned to smile at Mandie and then added, "I am riding my horse, but I will follow your carriage."

"Thank you. We're ready to go now," Mrs. Taft said as she rose. "Don't forget your cat, Amanda."

"Yes, Grandmother," Mandie said, ducking under the

table to untie Snowball's leash and pick him up.

As they approached their carriage outside, and Albert went to get his horse from the hitching rack, Celia exclaimed, "Oh, look! That beautiful stallion belongs to him! I wish I could ride it."

"Celia, that's a pretty big horse for a young girl like you," Jonathan said as the three climbed into the carriage and sat down.

"Oh, Jonathan, you forget that I was raised with horses. We have a horse farm in Virginia, you know . . ."

Mrs. Taft spoke to all of them, "Amanda, Celia, Jonathan, I want you to be on your best behavior at this house. We are not really going about this visit in a very proper manner. We should have been introduced to Mr. Van Dongen himself before we accepted the invitation."

"But, Grandmother, we have so little time here in Holland that we might never have met him properly," Mandie argued, holding Snowball in her lap. "Thank you so much for accepting Albert's invitation."

"Amanda! We are not on a first-name basis with these people. The young man's name is Mr. Van Dongen, just like his father," Mrs. Taft corrected.

"But, Grandmother, I don't believe he is much older than I am, even though he did say he had been to the port on his father's business," Mandie said.

"Nonetheless, we will at least stay proper in that respect, and you will all call him Mr. Van Dongen, unless he instructs you to use his first name," Mrs. Taft told Mandie and the others.

The three nodded their agreement.

As William drove their carriage down the country road, Mandie saw Albert riding alongside the carriage. Now and then he would look directly through the window at her and smile. She felt strangely uncomfortable. She had never experienced such a feeling toward a young man before. What was it about him that made her want to look away?

"It certainly was nice of Mr. Van Dongen to ask us home with him, wasn't it?" Celia remarked.

"Yes, it was," Mandie said. "I'm so anxious to see his father's windmill and find out about the position of the blades." She noticed that her grandmother was busy talking to the senator and was not paying attention to their conversation.

"Mandie, I think you are trying to ignore the fact that this Albert Van Dongen was instantly smitten with you," Jonathan teased, wearing his mischievous smile.

Mandie felt her face turn red as she tried to come up with an answer. "Jonathan Guyer, stop that!" she said, bending quickly to pet Snowball, who was sitting on the floor at her feet.

"Didn't you think it strange that he happened to be in the same eating place as we were?" Jonathan continued. "He probably put William up to recommending that inn so he could meet you there."

"Jonathan!" Mandie said angrily. "You are talking nonsense and I don't want to hear any more about it. Now we will only discuss the windmill, which is the only reason we're going to the miller's house."

"If you say so," Jonathan said, sitting back in his seat.

Mandie's mind was confused as they rode along. She wanted to ask the miller why the blades were in the unusual position they saw them in the night before. But her thoughts kept turning to his good-looking son, and then she would feel her face get warm again. She resolved she would ignore Albert when they got to his home and only talk to his father.

At that moment Albert rode by the window, smiling at her, and she wondered how she would ever be able to ignore him.

Chapter 6 / Mr. Van Dongen's Denial

William pulled their carriage up in front of what everyone had been calling "the miller's cottage." It looked like a mansion to Mandie compared with the house they were renting. Evidently being a miller must be a very lucrative occupation. And seeing the windmill up close, it was huge.

As the three young people stepped down from the vehicle behind Mrs. Taft and Senator Morton, Mandie suddenly found Albert standing by her side. He smiled at her and then spoke to Mrs. Taft, "Madam, if you will please, follow me. My father is at home doing bookwork. The mill is not operating today."

He opened a glass-paned front door and showed them into an elaborate parlor. It was very formal and very rich-looking, Mandie decided, done in hues of blue and green. Snowball squirmed to get down.

"No, no, Snowball, be still," Mandie scolded, holding him tightly in her arms.

"It is all right for him to get down," Albert said. "We also have a cat who runs loose in the house. I will bring him in to play with your cat." Turning to Mrs. Taft he said, "Madam, if you would please all take seats, I will get my father."

"Thank you," Mrs. Taft replied as everyone found a place to sit.

Albert smiled again at Mandie and quickly left the room. Mandie sat on a chair by the door, still holding Snowball in her lap.

"Did you notice the position of the windmill's blades?" Jonathan asked. "They were stopped at one-thirty, four-thirty, seven-thirty, and ten-thirty."

"Oh, no," Mandie said with a big sigh. "I plumb forgot with all the excitement of coming here."

"It is exciting to unexpectedly meet the miller's son, and then get invited right into his home, isn't it?" Celia said.

"I guess so, if you're a girl," Jonathan said with a grin.

"If you're jealous because Albert smiled at Celia and me, then maybe you should treat us more like *girls*," Mandie told him, her blue eyes twinkling. "We might love you for it."

The remark made Jonathan blush, just as Mandie figured it would. And she also felt they were even now when it came to teasing.

Celia smiled but didn't say a word.

At that moment Albert returned, saving Jonathan the need to answer Mandie.

Albert's father was with him, and Mandie saw at once that Albert was an exact younger duplicate of his father, right down to the smile.

Mr. Van Dongen stepped forward to take Mrs. Taft's hand and introduce himself before Albert had the chance.

"Madam, what a pleasure indeed," he said, bending to kiss her hand. "I am Albert Van Dongen, the same as my son, except I am the first and he is the second." He spoke with a clipped accent. "Welcome to my humble home."

"Thank you, Mr. Van Dongen. I do hope you'll forgive this sudden visit. Your son invited us, assuring us it would be all right," Mrs. Taft said, smiling up at the tall man. She introduced Senator Morton, and then the young people.

After exchanging greetings, Mr. Van Dongen sat down near the adults. "Albert, please make a seat for yourself," he told his son. As Albert sat down near Mandie and her friends, his father continued, "My son is so excited to meet people from the United States of America, because he will be going to school there when the next term opens."

"How wonderful!" Mrs. Taft enthused.

While the adults were occupied with their own conversation, Mandie was still having trouble with Snowball squirming in her arms, and at that moment he managed to escape. She grabbed for him but he raced to smell Albert's shoes, and then he jumped into the young man's lap.

"Oh, the cat! I forgot," Albert said, quickly standing up and placing Snowball on the floor. "I will get him," he said, leaving the room quickly.

"So he is going to the United States to school," Mandie said quietly to her friends. "I wonder what school, and where?"

"Ask him," Celia said.

"Oh, no, I couldn't do that," Mandie said, suddenly shy at the prospect.

"Why not?" Jonathan said, just as Albert returned with

a beautiful gray cat, much larger than Snowball. He sat him on the floor and the young people waited and watched to see how the two would react.

Snowball spit at the gray cat, which sat there staring at him. Then the white kitten slowly edged forward to smell the other cat. Albert's cat looked down its nose at Snowball until Snowball was just inches from him. Then he suddenly bristled his fur and began backing away. Snowball meowed and followed him.

Mandie laughed, "I believe your cat is afraid of mine," she told Albert.

Albert also laughed and said, "Not afraid. Surprised. It is the first time he has ever seen another cat that I know of."

The three young people looked at Albert in disbelief.

"He has never seen another cat? Don't you people have cats in Holland?" Mandie asked.

"Yes, lots of cats, but not in this house," Albert replied. He is not allowed to run loose. And the Widow DeWeese's cat died before we got this one. He was allowed in the mill because of rats."

"Did you say DeWeese? That's a family name in North Carolina where I come from," Mandie said.

"But this lady is from France. She is French," Albert said.

"Maybe the people back home by that name came from France," Mandie said, and then changing the subject, she asked, "Is your father going to show us the windmill?"

"Of course, after he makes your grandmother and the senator welcome," Albert explained.

Mandie noticed that Snowball and the gray cat had finally become friends and were rolling around on the floor. Mr. Van Dongen kept talking to her grandmother and the senator, and Mandie was feeling increasingly uncomfortable with Albert. His constant smiling at her made her feel embarrassed, because she knew Jonathan was watching.

Finally Mr. Van Dongen stopped talking to the adults and turned to converse with the young people. He moved to a chair nearer them, after excusing himself to Mrs. Taft.

"Welcome to my house," he said. "So you are Mrs. Taft's granddaughter, Amanda."

"Yes, sir, I am," Mandie said. "My friends call me Mandie for short. You have a beautiful home, Mr. Van Dongen."

The man glanced around, spread his hands and said, "Not like when my wife was living. The maid has no one to supervise her." He turned to look at Celia, "And you are Celia."

Celia smiled and nodded, "Yes, sir," she said. "Celia Hamilton. Mandie is my best friend."

"And you, young fellow, are the son of Mr. Lindall Guyer, whose family left Holland many, many years ago to live in the United States of America, I understand."

"You know my father, sir?" Jonathan asked in surprise.

"No, I do not know your father. I know *of* him," the man said, smiling.

Jonathan shrugged his shoulders and said, "Seems like everywhere we go someone knows my father's name."

"Yes, he is well known all over Europe. He is involved in so many business dealings, which are usually written about in the newspapers," Mr. Van Dongen explained.

"What kind of business dealings has my father had here in your country, Mr. Van Dongen?" Jonathan asked with great interest.

"Just a few weeks ago he contributed a large sum of money to a school our young Queen Wilhelmina has established for the poorer children. She is now a young woman of twenty-one and is interested in such work," Mr. Van Dongen explained.

Jonathan turned to explain to the girls: "Queen Wilhelmina became queen of the Netherlands at the age of ten when her father, William III, died."

The girls gasped. Mandie said to Mr. Van Dongen, "You had a ten-year-old girl ruling the country?"

Mr. Van Dongen smiled and explained, "It is not like the presidency of your country. Queen Wilhelmina's mother, Emma of Waldeck-Pyrmont, was regent until Wilhelmina became eighteen years old in 1898."

"Why couldn't her mother be the queen?" Mandie asked.

"Because the royal family descends on her father's side, not her mother's," Mr. Van Dongen said. "All the way back to William of Orange, the forefather of the royal family."

Mrs. Taft spoke from across the room, "Amanda, we will be going to Delft to the Delftware factory. Delft is called the City of Princes and was also the city of William of Orange."

Mandie asked, "Will we be able to see Queen Wilhelmina, Grandmother?"

Mrs. Taft smiled and said, "No, dear, I'm afraid we aren't acquainted with the queen."

"If you stay long enough you will most likely see the queen in some public event," Mr. Van Dongen told Mandie.

Mandie shook her head and said, "We're only here for a short visit. We have to go on to Ireland."

"Yes, you see, I have been taking the young people

on a tour of Europe, and in order to see a lot of countries we can't spend much time in any particular place," Mrs. Taft explained. "We still have Ireland, Scotland, Wales, and England to visit. Then we have to rush home for the young people to get into school on time."

"Then you must return to our country and plan to stay longer next time," Mr. Van Dongen told Mrs. Taft. "We would be honored to have you all as our guests here in our home."

"Thank you, Mr. Van Dongen. Maybe we will some time," Mrs. Taft said.

"That's very gracious of you, sir," Senator Morton said.

Mandie was getting impatient with the conversation. All she wanted to do was see the windmill and ask the miller about the setting of the blades the night before. She kept looking at her friends, who only shook their heads slightly.

Suddenly Mandie made a decision. She bent slightly toward Albert and said softly, "The windmill, please."

"Of course, of course," Albert quickly replied. He stood up and looked at his father. "Pardon the intrusion, Papa, but Mandie and Celia and Jonathan would like to see the windmill, if you will allow me to show it to them."

Mr. Van Dongen immediately apologized to Mrs. Taft. "I am sorry for the delay in seeing the windmill."

"Oh, no, sir, I have seen quite a few windmills in my lifetime, and I'm sure the senator has also; so with your permission, please allow the young people to go ahead with your son, Albert," Mrs. Taft replied.

"Yes, yes," Senator Morton agreed.

"You may go, then, Albert, but be careful. Our young guests are not familiar with the mechanism of the windmill," Mr. Van Dongen cautioned.

"Yes, sir," Albert said.

"We'll be fine," Mandie told her grandmother, who eyed her carefully. As the young people stood to leave, Mandie suddenly remembered her kitten. "Albert, should I take Snowball with me?"

"Of course, and I will take our cat," Albert said, bending to pick up the huge gray animal.

"Doesn't your cat have a name?" Mandie asked as she reached for Snowball.

"Oh, yes, his name is Flour Rat," Albert said as they walked toward the door of the room.

The three young people stopped and laughed, and Mandie said, "Flour Rat? What a name for a cat."

"He has earned it," Albert explained as he led the way through the house. "He keeps the rats out of our flour. He is an intelligent animal."

Mandie looked at her friends and smiled behind Albert's back.

As they entered the huge room that turned out to be the flour mill, Albert showed them the mechanism that was turned by the revolving blades of the windmill.

"Of course you must know that the wind turns the blades. The sails are made of lightweight canvas, and once the wind strikes them they rotate very fast," Albert said. "The wheat is ground and sifted here, and the finished result is the flour over there in the barrels."

The young people listened to every word, and Mandie's mind traveled through the operation. Back home in the North Carolina mountains where she came from, people used waterwheels for such work. And the Cherokees beat the wheat grain by hand to dislodge the meal that made the flour. The windmill was something different to see.

Albert put Flour Rat down, and the cat immediately

began poking around the floor. Snowball was squirming to join him.

"It is all right if Snowball joins Flour Rat," Albert said with a smile at Mandie.

Mandie hesitated. The mill was huge and Snowball could find plenty of hiding places. "Well, I'll let him down on his leash," she said as she put the kitten on the floor and held tightly to the end of his red leash. "He runs away every chance he gets."

"The doors are closed. He cannot get outside," Albert assured her.

Mandie decided it was time to ask the question about the position of the blades the night before. She looked up at Albert and said, "We lost Snowball last night because someone left our door open. We had gone for a walk to look at your windmill, and when we got back to the house he was gone. Did you know the blades on your windmill were in the wrong position last night?"

"In the wrong position?" Albert asked, puzzled.

"Yes. It was late, probably near midnight, and the blades were not set to show the mill was closed," Mandie tried to explain. "And when we looked back, the blades suddenly moved and stopped at the one-thirty, four-thirty, seven-thirty, and ten-thirty positions, which we understand shows the mill is closed."

"You are right about that, but my father retired before dark last night and set the blades accordingly," Albert told her.

"But we all saw the blades move," Jonathan joined in.

"Yes, we did," Celia agreed.

Albert suggested, "Perhaps the moonlight caused the blades to look as though they were moving. My father and I were both at home. We didn't retire until my sister came in around midnight."

Mandie was insistent. "I'm sorry to disagree with you, but we all three saw the position of the blades, and then saw them move to indicate the mill was closed," she told Albert, looking straight into his blue eyes.

Albert flushed slightly and said, "I think that we should give your information to my father and see what he has to say."

Jonathan spoke up and said, "Yes. He might have moved the blades without your knowing about it."

"We thought the wrong position of the blades may be a distress signal or something," Celia told the young man.

Albert looked at each one of the young people, then stooped to pick up Flour Rat. "Let us go see my father," he said, sounding rather serious.

With Snowball racing along at the end of his leash Mandie followed Albert back to the house. Celia and Jonathan were close behind.

Mr. Van Dongen was still in the parlor with Mrs. Taft and Senator Morton. They seemed to be discussing Holland's flower parades. The young people paused in the doorway.

"It's such a gift to be able to fabricate animals and objects out of flowers for the parade," Mrs. Taft was saying. "And the participants are so talented, moving so gracefully with all those flowers covering them from head to foot."

"And the sweet scent of roses is enough to make an old man want to turn to young romance again," Senator Morton said with a little laugh.

Jonathan looked at Mandie and grinned as he whispered, "Better watch out for your grandmother. Romeo has come alive again."

Mandie poked his side with her elbow as she advanced into the parlor.

Mr. Van Dongen looked up as they entered the room. "Did Albert give you a nice visit of our windmill?" he asked them.

"Yes, sir," they all replied.

"But, Mr. Van Dongen, we have a problem," Mandie said, walking up to the settee where he was sitting. "Or I should say we have a disagreement."

"A disagreement? Well now, Albert, what have you been disagreeable about?" Mr. Van Dongen asked. "Sit down and tell me, all of you."

"Let Mandie tell you," Albert said, setting his cat down on the carpet and motioning for Mandie to go ahead.

Mrs. Taft and Senator Morton sat in rapt attention as Mandie and her two friends sat on a settee nearby. Albert flopped onto a footstool in front of them.

"Well, you see, Mr. Van Dongen, last night Celia and Jonathan and I went for a walk to see your windmill," Mandie began as Snowball curled up at her feet. "We didn't know how to get across the canal, so that was as far as we went. But, mind you, the moon was shining. Therefore we could clearly see the blades on your windmill." She paused to look at Albert and then quickly added, "And they were definitely in the wrong position. We all three noticed it. And when we started back we turned to look one more time at the windmill, and suddenly the blades moved into the right place to indicate the mill was closed for the night." She blew out her breath and waited to see what Mr. Van Dongen would say.

The Dutchman's face flushed fiery red as he dropped his gaze and replied, "Those blades could not have been in the wrong position. I set them myself when I closed the mill before dark. You must be mistaken."

Mandie heard Mrs. Taft gasp as the miller's tone of voice became harsh.

"But, sir, we all three saw the position of the blades and then saw them move. If it had been only one of us, you might believe us to be mistaken, but we all saw everything," Jonathan insisted.

"Yes, we did," Celia agreed.

The old man shook his head.

Mandie suddenly remembered the figure in the dark and said, "We also saw someone among the flower bushes, and he ran away from us. Actually, we couldn't be sure if it was a man or a woman."

Mr. Van Dongen looked at her and asked, "Someone ran away from you? And you couldn't tell whether it was a man or a woman?"

"It was too dark, sir," Mandie replied. "But if I hadn't gotten my skirt tangled in the rosebushes, we could have caught him, or at least seen more clearly who it was."

"If it was too dark to see whether it was a man or a woman, then how could you see the position of the blades on the windmill?" Mr. Van Dongen asked with a frown.

"The moon was shining directly on the windmill, but the person we saw was stooping low among the flowers, trying to hide from us," Mandie explained.

"Probably some servant out on a lark when he should have been home," Mr. Van Dongen muttered. He looked directly at Mandie and said firmly, "And I assure you that you were all mistaken about the position of the windmill's blades." He stood up. "Now, I am sorry, but I must get back to my work on the books." He bowed slightly to Mrs. Taft.

"Of course, Mr. Van Dongen," Mrs. Taft said as she and Senator Morton both quickly rose. "I apologize for dropping in on you unexpectedly like this. We appreciate your hospitality and kindness."

"And you must come back before you leave our country," the Dutchman said. "Albert will show your driver the way across the canal. Good day." He brusquely left the room.

Albert smiled at Mrs. Taft and said, "We will find your carriage at the front, I believe." He led the group out the front door, smiled at Mandie, and asked them all to return to visit. He then stood watching as they all climbed into the carriage and rode away.

Mandie and her friends sat in silence for a few moments. Mandie felt that Mr. Van Dongen was angry with them because they had asked about the windmill blades, but she couldn't figure out why. As William drove them back to the house, Mrs. Taft and the senator spoke quietly with each other as though nothing unusual had happened.

"Mr. Van Dongen was so nice and friendly, until we mentioned the windmill blades," Mandie finally remarked quietly. "Then he acted angry with us, like he wanted us to hurry up and leave."

"That's what I thought, too," Jonathan said.

"I thought it was very discourteous of him to suddenly say he had to go back to work," Celia said.

"Yes, and did you notice that Albert didn't have one word to say after we went back to the house and told his father about last night?" Mandie remarked.

"I don't think he believed us, either," Jonathan said.

"Neither one of them wanted to believe us. It was almost as if they had some secret reason to dispute everything we said," Mandie added.

"Like what, Mandie?" Celia asked.

"Like maybe the blades were set in that odd position for a certain reason, and they knew about it but didn't want us to know," Mandie said as Snowball settled down around her feet.

"Did you notice the way Mr. Van Dongen passed off your remark about seeing someone in the flowers last night?" Jonathan asked.

"Yes, and I think we ought to find out why," Mandie announced.

"But, Mandie!" Celia exclaimed under her breath. "That's not our business."

"We'll make it our business to find out who that person was last night, and why the windmill's blades were in the wrong position and then suddenly moved to normal," Mandie said. "It shouldn't be so hard to find out."

Jonathan and Celia looked at each other and sighed.

Chapter 7 / Who Mixed the Paint?

The young people were tired from their late-night escapades the night before, and made no objection when Mrs. Taft sent everyone off to bed early. It seemed to Mandie that she had just gone to sleep when Gretchen was knocking on the door to say that breakfast was ready.

"We'll be down in a few minutes," Mandie called sleepily to the maid. She shook Celia awake, and they both jumped out of bed. Snowball tumbled to the floor.

"Do not be too long or the food will be cold," Gretchen replied through the closed door as she hurried on down the hallway.

Mandie yawned and stretched while she reached for a dress in the tall wardrobe. "I didn't wake up at all last night. And I didn't dream either," she told Celia.

Celia also pulled a fresh garment down for herself. "Me either," she said. "I suppose our late night has finally caught up to us."

"Yes, but now we have to be alert for every chance

we get to begin working on our mystery," Mandie said, slipping on a pale pink linen dress.

"But, Mandie, there is no way we can find out who that was we saw in the flower field, or who set the windmill blades," Celia said as she straightened her long tan skirt. "If you ask me, I believe Mr. Van Dongen is the one who set the blades and then moved them." She stuffed a yellow linen waist into the band of her skirt.

Mandie twirled before the mirror, and then looked at her friend. "You do? Why?"

"Well, he acted strange when we told him everything," Celia said, coming to stand by Mandie in front of the looking glass. "In fact, I think he was angry that we knew about the blades, and that we saw someone in the flowers."

"Yes, he was," Mandie admitted again. "That's why I think it is some kind of a secret, and he doesn't want us to find out anything more. Remember that Albert did not say anything to defend us before his father?"

"Yes," Celia replied, then added with a smile, "And that is strange, because he seemed really smitten with you. You ought to use that to your advantage."

Mandie felt a blush rise in her cheeks. "Smitten? You sound like Jonathan. Whatever in the world are you talking about, Celia Hamilton?"

"Oh, Mandie, you know he is definitely interested in you. Why, he didn't take his eyes off you all the time we were there," Celia said. "You could very easily influence him into talking to his father about this whole thing for us."

Mandie thought for a moment as a frown crossed her brow. "You're right, Celia. I might see what I can do if I get a chance," she said.

"But right now we'd better get on down to breakfast," Celia reminded her.

Mandie bent to fasten Snowball's leash onto his collar.

"I'll ask Gretchen to feed Snowball while we eat, because I'm going to have to take him with us. We'll probably be gone all day, and I just can't leave him shut up here that long," she said.

"I'll help you take care of him while we're out, Mandie," Celia offered.

"Thanks. You always do and I appreciate it," Mandie told her as they started for the door.

Everyone else was already at the table when the girls entered the dining room. Gretchen took Snowball, and Mandie and Celia sat down.

"Celia and I both were still asleep when Gretchen knocked on our door," Mandie told her grandmother.

"So was I, dear," she admitted. "I suppose we were all tired out. We've done nothing but travel and gad about for such a long time now," Mrs. Taft replied.

Gretchen had come back and was pouring the coffee. Hot rolls were on the table.

"Now that everyone is here I'll get the food," Gretchen told Mrs. Taft and left the room.

"Sleepy heads," Jonathan teased the girls. "I've been up since the crack of dawn."

"And what have you been doing since then?" Mandie asked as she sipped her cup of hot coffee.

"I've been out to look at the windmill," Jonathan told her.

"Did you go all the way over there?" Mandie asked, surprised.

"Oh, no. I just walked far enough around the house to see the position of the blades," Jonathan explained.

Mandie waited for him to go on, but he merely sat there smiling mischievously at her.

"Well, where were the blades stopped?" Mandie asked in an exasperated voice.

"Now that you've asked, they were in the regular closed-for-the-night position," Jonathan said, and then added with a grin, "Nothing exciting. All normal."

"Jonathan, sometimes I could shake you," Mandie muttered so that her grandmother at the end of the table could not hear her.

"That goes for me, too. Sometimes you are overly aggressive," Jonathan replied, sipping his coffee and reaching for a roll.

Mandie took a deep breath and said, "Now that we're even, let's get on with our mystery. Did you see Albert or his father?"

"No one, not even the cat, but then Albert said the cat was not allowed to run outside," Jonathan replied.

Mrs. Taft spoke from the end of the table as Gretchen brought in the food, "Amanda, Celia, Jonathan, eat up now. We must hurry to get to Delft this morning so that we might have time for something else today."

"Yes, ma'am," Mandie replied, helping herself to the dishes of hot food being passed.

"Mandie, if we see Albert today, don't forget what I told you," Celia reminded Mandie of their earlier conversation in their room.

"I won't," Mandie assured her.

Jonathan quickly looked at the girls and asked, "What do you mean by that?"

"Nothing you would understand," Mandie said with a smile.

"I may not understand everything that goes on, but remember I'm always right there with you girls, and if you see Albert I'll see him, too," Jonathan replied.

"Please discontinue your conversation and concentrate on your food. We need to get going," Mrs. Taft told the young people.

The three replied, "Yes, ma'am," and hurriedly cleaned their plates.

"If you will excuse me, I will see about our carriage," Senator Morton told Mrs. Taft as he rose to leave the table.

"Of course, thank you, Senator," Mrs. Taft replied as the senator left the room.

"If you will excuse me also, I'll go help," Jonathan said to Mrs. Taft.

"Go ahead, Jonathan. We'll be along soon," Mrs. Taft said as she finished her coffee. Jonathan quickly left the room.

Mandie, suspicious of Jonathan's motive for leaving, quickly swallowed the last bite on her plate and said, "I'm finished, Grandmother."

"I am also," Celia added.

"Well, then, it looks like we're all finished, so let's get started," Mrs. Taft said as she pushed back her chair.

Gretchen, standing nearby, told Mandie, "I'll get your cat," and left the room.

"Are you planning on taking your cat with you today, Amanda?" Mrs. Taft asked.

"I have to, Grandmother. We'll probably be gone all day, and I can't leave him shut up all alone in our room that long," Mandie said as Gretchen returned with Snowball in her arms and handed him to his mistress.

"Be sure you watch after him carefully, then. I won't have time wasted because of that cat running away and getting into things," Mrs. Taft warned her.

"I'm going to help her with Snowball," Celia said as the three left the dining room.

William had the carriage waiting at the front door while Senator Morton stood by. Mandie looked around, but couldn't see Jonathan anywhere.

"Where is Jonathan, Senator Morton?" Mandie asked.

"He said he wanted to walk around the house a minute for something," the senator told her.

"I'll go get him," Mandie said, giving her cat to Celia in a hurry, and rushing off down the pathway before her grandmother could object.

She found him exactly where she expected. He was standing down in the flower field looking at the windmill in the distance.

"Jonathan Guyer, we are fixing to leave you," she called to him.

Jonathan quickly turned and started walking toward her. "I just wanted to see if the blades on the windmill had changed position."

Mandie glanced at the blades across the field. They were still in the closed position as far as she could tell. Evidently Mr. Van Dongen didn't get up and go to work very early.

"You see they haven't moved," Jonathan told her as he caught up with her in the pathway.

"You know Grandmother is in a hurry, so come on," Mandie told him as she hurried back around the house.

Mrs. Taft, Senator Morton, and Celia, with Snowball, were already in the carriage, and Mandie rushed up to join them. She looked at her grandmother as she quickly sat down next to Celia, and Jonathan practically tumbled in beside her in his haste. Mrs. Taft didn't seem to notice that the two had delayed their start a few minutes.

"Tell us about this place we're going to visit, Grandmother," Mandie said as William got the carriage on its way.

"It's an ancient city. As I've said before, it is called the City of William of Orange, who was the father of the Dutch Royal family," Mrs. Taft began. "I'm sure you will all be fascinated with the town. It's so old and quaint."

"What about the Delftware factory?" Mandie asked.

"I believe it was along about the beginning of the seventeenth century that the Dutch were being put out of the porcelain business by Chinese imports," Mrs. Taft said. "The Chinese had learned how to make probably the best porcelain in the world. Well, the Royal family had to do something about this. So the Dutch people learned how to make the Delft blue ware, which was done by hand and exquisitely painted. And the Delftware surpassed its Eastern counterpart."

"So all the porcelain is blue?" Mandie asked.

"Well, the Delftware is white, but the painting on it is all blue," Mrs. Taft answered.

After a long journey they finally arrived at the city of Delft. The young people watched out the window of the carriage as they passed canals, steep bridges, and old houses with quaint gables and tile roofs. There seemed to be sidewalk cafes everywhere and several open-air markets.

"Oh, this is so interesting!" Mandie exclaimed as she looked at the scenery. Snowball woke up and stretched at her feet.

"We will be stopping at a cafe to get some refreshments first, then we'll go on to the factory," Mrs. Taft told them.

"I could sure use some refreshment," Jonathan said with a sigh. "I guess I didn't eat enough breakfast."

"Me, either," Celia added.

"I can smell the food already," Mandie said as the odor of freshly baked bread drifted through the carriage windows.

"I asked William to let us out at the next square, I believe," Senator Morton told Mrs. Taft. "There's a place on the corner that has good food."

After they left the carriage, Mrs. Taft allowed them to

walk about the area for a few minutes. Mandie put Snowball on his leash. She and Senator Morton kept right up with them. The young people were excited over the picturesque village. Everywhere they looked they saw something that held their interest.

"Oh, I'd like to stay here awhile!" Mandie exclaimed as they walked over a high, steep bridge made of stone, surrounded by flowers.

"Unfortunately we have to return to our house tonight," Mrs. Taft told her. "We can't get too far behind with our schedule for the other countries."

As the young people stepped off the curved bridge, Mandie suddenly saw a flash of a familiar face in the crowd. She knew immediately that it was the woman from the ship who had been following them everywhere they went.

"Quick! The woman from the ship!" she called to her friends. Picking up Snowball she raced off in the direction the woman had gone.

Jonathan and Celia quickly followed, while Mrs. Taft and Senator Morton stood there wondering what had caused the young people to hurry away.

Mandie searched the crowd, looking behind statues, bushes, and fences, but she couldn't find a sign of the woman. She stopped and stomped her foot as her friends caught up with her.

"She got away, as usual," Mandie told them. "But I'm sure it was that strange woman from the ship. I do wish she would quit following us everywhere."

"I think we just ought to ignore her if we see her again," Celia said.

"Yes, she's always playing games with us, running away like that," Jonathan agreed.

"But we don't know why she does it," Mandie said.

With a final look around she said, "Guess we'd better go back. Grandmother will wonder what we're doing."

As they returned to where she and Senator Morton were waiting, Mrs. Taft asked, "Amanda, what possessed you to run off like that?"

"Sorry, Grandmother, I thought I saw someone I knew," Mandie told her.

"Someone you knew? Here in Holland? How could that be?" Mrs. Taft asked.

"Well, I guess it wasn't," Mandie said, deciding not to discuss the strange woman with her grandmother. "I'm starving. Could we eat now?"

"Just be sure that we all stay together from now on," Mrs. Taft said as she and Senator Morton led the way to the sidewalk cafe. White tables and chairs were arranged in clusters on a blue and white tile floor. Pots full of blooming plants outlined the dining area. And the smell of food was enough to make the young people ravenous.

"We can't spend too much time here," Mrs. Taft reminded them. "So decide quickly what you want to order."

With Senator Morton to guide them through the Dutch menu, the young people finally ordered a delicious meal of creamed chicken. Mandie tied Snowball to the table leg and fed him a small dish of food when it came.

Within a short time they were all ready to travel on to the factory. The road was winding and narrow, and they crossed a steep bridge over a small canal. When the factory came within sight, Mandie was somewhat disappointed with the look of it. It was very old and was surrounded with crumbling stone walls. It looked more like a fortress than a factory.

"It certainly is a strange-looking factory," Mandie remarked as they alighted. She left Snowball in the carriage.

"Wait until you get inside," Mrs. Taft remarked, "and

you'll see such wonderful work being done that you'll forget about the way the place looks."

One door was open to visitors, and they had to get into a line before going inside. Mandie noticed several different nationalities in the crowd, and could hear various languages being spoken.

Senator Morton explained: "You will see visitors from many countries here. It is famous worldwide, and a visit to Holland is not complete without a visit here."

The young people played a guessing game as to the nationalities represented. "That blond man and woman ahead of us are probably Swedish," Jonathan said quietly.

Mandie asked, "How can you tell?"

"I can hear them talking," Jonathan said with a grin.

Mandie glanced behind them and saw an Oriental man and woman join the line.

"And I imagine those people behind us are Chinese," she said smugly.

Jonathan turned discreetly to look. "You are probably right," he agreed.

"I've never seen Chinese people before, but they look like the pictures I've seen," Celia agreed as she stole a glance.

The line moved forward quickly, and they found themselves inside the structure with Mrs. Taft and Senator Morton. Aisles were roped off so that the visitors could walk along and watch the workers without interrupting them. A tall Dutchman herded them along, but no information was given. It seemed to be a case of watch and see for yourself.

They passed huge vats of blue paint and then yellow paint. Mandie wondered what they did with the yellow paint if the porcelain was all painted blue.

"What do they do with the yellow paint?" she finally asked.

"Well, I don't know," Jonathan began, "but if we dumped some of this yellow into the blue paint over there we'd have green."

Mandie was shocked. "Jonathan Guyer, how dare you even say such a thing!" she exclaimed. "It would ruin everything!"

"And cause all sorts of trouble," Celia added.

"Of course it would. I didn't really intend doing that," Jonathan said, alarmed that the girls thought he was serious. "I just don't know what they do with the yellow paint."

Senator Morton heard this remark and turned back to say, "Look at the wall over in that corner. It looks like they are painting it yellow."

The young people looked in the direction he pointed and saw that he was right. Fresh yellow paint covered part of the wall.

After the adults drifted a little ahead, Jonathan whispered to the girls, "I'd still like to see what would happen if we mixed the blue and the yellow."

"You'd better not try it," Mandie cautioned as they moved forward.

The paint seemed to be coming through funnels at each worker's table, and as they watched, the blue design was carefully painted on the porcelain. Mandie was fascinated by it all, until she suddenly realized Jonathan had disappeared.

"Where did Jonathan go?" Mandie whispered to Celia.

"I don't know," Celia said, looking about for him.

"Come along, Amanda," Mrs. Taft called back to her.

Then as easily as Jonathan had disappeared, he suddenly turned up in line again without the girls seeing where he'd come from.

"Jonathan, where have you been?" Mandie whispered to him.

"That's a secret," Jonathan replied with his mischievous grin.

Mandie frowned at him and moved along quickly behind the adults. There were a lot of people in line and it was slow-moving, but Mandie enjoyed watching the workers fashion the blue designs with their swift strokes.

Suddenly a worker that she was watching cried out. She looked to see what was wrong. A man who was evidently the supervisor came running to the worker's table. There was a lot of excited talk back and forth, and Mandie strained to see over heads. Finally she found an opening to peek through. She could see that the worker's design was green instead of blue!

Turning quickly, Mandie stomped on Jonathan's foot and said, "Jonathan, you mixed the blue and the yellow! How could you?"

Jonathan looked shocked as he said, "No, I didn't!" He looked at Mandie and then at the piece of porcelain the worker was holding.

The adults turned to see what the commotion was about. Mandie immediately straightened up and stopped accusing Jonathan. It would be better if her grandmother didn't know what Jonathan had done.

Mrs. Taft looked over at the three and then said to the senator, "Can you imagine what kind of person would do such a thing? To ruin all that paint and porcelain?"

"I'd say it would be a very dangerous thing to do with all the possible repercussions from the Royal family. This factory is their pride and joy," Senator Morton replied.

Someone seemed to be shoving in line behind them, so Mandie turned to look back. Some people were leaving without finishing the tour. She noticed an older couple walking toward the doorway they had come through, and the Oriental man and woman were also leaving. Then the people ahead of them, that Jonathan had said were Swedish, also turned to go back the way they had come in.

"Come along, Amanda," Mrs. Taft urged.

Mandie looked forward to see the room suddenly fill with guards who were ushering the people out another doorway. Evidently they had been in the building all the time.

As they stepped outside, one of the guards was asking for identification and writing information on a tablet. Senator Morton took care of all their papers and the man passed them on. They were free to leave.

As they walked toward their waiting carriage, Mrs. Taft discussed the matter with Senator Morton. The young people, following closely, listened. Mandie kept watching Jonathan out of the corner of her eye. He seemed to be watching the other visitors.

"That was certainly a stroke of bad luck for us, as well as for the factory," Mrs. Taft remarked. "We didn't get to see everything."

"Yes, and I hope they catch whoever did such a thing," Senator Morton replied. "The Royal family feel so strongly about this factory, I wouldn't be surprised if the culprit were hanged, if he is caught."

Mandie's heart thumped wildly in her chest. She knew Jonathan had done this awful thing, and now his very life would be in danger if he were found out. Well, she wouldn't go so far as to tell on him. She wouldn't want to be responsible for having him hung. But she would keep her eyes open for any more such deeds he might try to do, because she was determined not to be involved in such things.

Chapter 8 / Where Are the Van Dongens?

As they stood waiting for William to bring their carriage alongside the narrow pathway outside the Delftware factory, Mandie noticed the Chinese man and woman standing nearby talking to the older couple who had been in line inside. She couldn't understand the language they were speaking, and she frowned as she watched them. The Chinese man happened to glance her way, and suddenly the strangers all changed their conversation to English.

"Yes, I hope they catch the terrible person who mixed that blue and yellow paint," the Chinese man was saying.

The other strangers in the group had turned to look at Mandie and her friends. The older man replied to the Chinese man, "Not only is it costly, it could damage the Dutch reputation for fine porcelain."

"And that must be maintained under all circumstances," the Chinese man said, glancing at Mandie again.

Mandie nudged Celia and Jonathan, who were also aware of the conversation among the strangers. "They keep looking to see if we're listening," she whispered.

Jonathan suddenly rolled off a few sentences in what Mandie recognized as French. Then he turned his back on the strangers, winked at the girls, and said softly, "I'm trying to make them think we're French."

"Jonathan, I'd advise you to behave yourself for the rest of the trip," Mandie admonished him with a frown. "No more fooling around."

Jonathan looked sharply at Mandie, sighed, and stepped ahead to stand by Mrs. Taft.

William came along with their carriage at that moment, and as they all climbed inside, Mandie, who usually sat between her two friends, gave Celia a little push to put her between Jonathan and herself.

Snowball, waiting in the carriage for his mistress, quickly jumped in her lap.

But William didn't get very far because another flower parade was passing by and he had to bring the carriage to a halt.

"M-m-m-m! I smell them!" Mandie exclaimed as she leaned out the window.

"Roses!" Celia added as she bent beside Mandie.

Jonathan kept his seat, and when Mandie glanced back at him, he said, "One flower parade is enough. When you've seen one you've seen them all."

Mandie looked back out the window and quickly answered, "You may be right. But I see that girl and young man we saw leave the other parade when we first got to Holland. See? Right over there." She tried to point at the moving participants.

Jonathan ignored her remark, but Celia said, excitedly, "You're absolutely correct, Mandie. They *are* the ones we saw."

"Maybe the same people participate in all the parades," Mandie said as the procession passed on and she sat back in her seat. She looked at Jonathan and he quickly glanced out the other window.

Senator Morton spoke to the young people: "That parade originated here at the factory. I saw them assembling behind the building when we went inside."

"I didn't notice," Mandie said, and then asked, "Where are we going now?"

Senator Morton looked at Mrs. Taft, who answered Mandie's question. "I thought we'd just go back to the house and relax for the rest of the day, dear," she said. "This excursion turned out to be far more tiring than I expected."

Mandie was instantly relieved. She was more interested in pursuing mysteries than in sight-seeing. "I'm sorry, Grandmother, if we've worn you out, but I think it's a good idea to quit for the day. After all, we never know when Uncle Ned might arrive, or when Senator Morton might get a message from Jonathan's father or his aunt and uncle," she said quickly.

Mrs. Taft smiled at her granddaughter and said, "Yes, I suppose you young people would rather go your own way than sight-see with us older folks."

"Oh, I've enjoyed seeing the sights with you folks," Jonathan insisted.

"And we've enjoyed having you with us, Jonathan," Senator Morton said.

"Yes, Jonathan, we are so glad you could join us for this journey around Europe," Mrs. Taft added.

Mandie was silent as she thought, *Grandmother doesn't know what Jonathan did back at the Delftware factory, or she'd be ready to wire his father to come and get him right now. But I'm not going to tell, be-*

*cause of what the Dutch people might do to him if he's
caught.*

When they finally arrived back at their rented house,
it was late in the day. Mrs. Taft immediately went to her
rooms, and Senator Morton left for a stroll after checking
with Gretchen to find there were no messages.

Mrs. Taft had warned the young people not to get into
any mischief. "Well, what do we do now?" Jonathan
asked as he sat across from the girls in the parlor.

"Do? Like what?" Mandie asked with a sarcastic
frown.

"You girls were planning to see Albert about something," Jonathan said in a long-drawn-out voice. "And I
suppose you two will want to pursue the so-called mysteries you've concocted."

"Jonathan Guyer, we didn't *make up* any mysteries
and you know it," Mandie said angrily. "You've been with
us when everything happened."

"Sure I've been with you, but I don't see the mystery
in these things, not really," Jonathan replied, raising his
dark eyebrows.

Mandie sighed and said, "You don't have to go along
with Celia and me if you don't want to, then, but there
are some questions I'm going to find the answers to."
She stood up and added, "Right now I'm going to find
Albert and ask him some questions." She picked up
Snowball and started toward the door.

Jonathan jumped up quickly and said, "Albert? Then
I'm going with you."

Celia followed as she asked, "But, Mandie, that's a
long way to walk. Remember, we have to go out of the
way in order to cross the canal."

"I know, Celia, but we'll make it back in time for supper if we hurry," Mandie said. She led the way, and her
friends rushed after her.

Snowball squirmed as his mistress held him tightly in one arm, and with her other hand lifted her long skirt. She raced through the flower fields toward the steep, curved bridge that crossed the canal. As she ran and the windmill came into view, she noticed the blades were set for closing and she wondered if the miller had ever gone to work that day. They were in the same position as they had been that morning.

The wind blew Mandie's bonnet back, and it hung from her neck by its ribbon. Her blonde hair tumbled free from its braid and fluttered about her face. But her thoughts were only on Albert. She believed he had the answers to the puzzles, and she intended to find out what he knew.

The house looked deserted and no one answered her knock. Celia and Jonathan stood by and waited while Mandie let Snowball down on his leash.

"I don't believe anyone is at home," Mandie finally said. She looked around the surrounding yard and then to the windmill nearby. There was no one in sight. Turning she said, "Let's look inside the windmill. Maybe someone is there."

But they soon found that was not possible. The windmill was locked.

"You'd think at least a servant would be around," Mandie said with a sigh. "And I remember Mr. Van Dongen mentioning a maid."

"But she may be only a day maid, Mandie," Celia said. "It's getting late."

"And I don't want to miss supper. I think I'll head back," Jonathan said, glancing for a response from Mandie as she stood in front of the door to the windmill.

"Well, let's go eat supper and come back over here later," Mandie said matter-of-factly. She picked up her kitten and led the way back to the house they were renting.

The three walked and then ran. There was no time for conversation if they were going to get back in time to dress for supper. When they arrived, Gretchen was looking for them. She met them at the front door.

"Food will be on the table in thirty minutes. Madam Taft has been notified," the girl said.

Mandie smiled at the maid's accent. "Thank you, Gretchen. We'll be there on time."

"See you girls at the table," Jonathan told them, and quickly ran up the steps.

Mandie and Celia went to their room, where they quickly changed into fresh clothes.

"I'm so sorry Jonathan has disappointed us with his behavior," Mandie remarked as she slipped the pale blue dress over her blonde head.

Celia stopped straightening her long skirt to look at her friend. "But, Mandie, we don't know for sure that Jonathan is guilty of mixing the blue and yellow paint at the Delftware factory. We didn't actually see him do it."

"But, Celia, he was talking about what would happen if he did," Mandie said, continuing with her sash. "I'm sure he did it. Besides, who else could have done it if he didn't?"

"Lots of people were in that room with us," Celia said. "In fact, people from several different countries."

"I just don't understand why no one saw the paint being mixed," Mandie said, bending to slip into her dress slippers. "I didn't even see Jonathan leave the line and then come back. That's how easy it was to do something out of the ordinary. And Jonathan acts guilty. He doesn't have anything to say since I accused him of mixing the paint."

"That's no proof he did it," Celia argued. "Look at it this way. If you accused me of doing something wrong, and I knew good and well I didn't do it, I wouldn't have much to say to you either. My feelings would be hurt."

Mandie thought about that a moment as she looked at Celia. She didn't have any proof that Jonathan had done such a thing, only the feeling that he was guilty because of his remarks about the blue and yellow paints before it happened.

"Well, if you think he didn't do it, then tell me where you think he went when he left the line," Mandie said, twirling to flounce out the frills on her long, organdy skirt. "When I asked him, he wouldn't tell me."

Celia frowned and said, "You know Jonathan. He likes to move around all the time. He might have just walked around to the other end of the room looking at everything and everybody."

"He told me it was a secret about where he'd been," Mandie told her.

"Well, he is a big tease. He was probably just teasing you," Celia decided. "Anyway, let me remind you of what Uncle Ned would say. He'd tell you to *think*."

"I'll talk to Uncle Ned about it when he gets here, if he ever does. Seems like he should have finished with his business in other places by now. Maybe he's visiting friends," Mandie said. Changing the subject, she asked, "Are you going back to the miller's house with me after supper?"

"Do you think your grandmother will allow us to go?" Celia asked.

"If she doesn't have any plans, I don't see why she wouldn't allow us to go over there. After all, she has already met the miller and his son and been in their house," Mandie said.

"Let's don't wait too late to go, Mandie," Celia said. "I don't think we should stay up all hours of the night wandering around."

Mandie smiled at her friend. "But that's what makes solving mysteries exciting. We'll go as soon after supper as possible."

When the girls went down to the dining room everyone was already there. Mandie handed Snowball to Gretchen so she could give him his supper. Then she sat down beside Celia, with Jonathan on the other side of her friend. She was determined not to be on a friendly basis with Jonathan until the mystery of the paint was solved.

No one had much to say at the supper table, but as soon as they were all finished, Mrs. Taft decided they would all go for a stroll in the flower gardens.

"We need some slow, relaxing exercise, so I thought we'd just walk in the gardens around the house for a little while," Mrs. Taft told the young people. "Then before we go to bed, maybe we'll have a cup of tea in the parlor. How does that sound to y'all?"

The three young people exchanged glances. Mandie raised her eyebrows slightly and said, "All right, Grandmother." She was hoping this wouldn't take long, but if it included tea afterward, it would probably be dark before they could return to the miller's house, and she decided not to even mention it. Somehow she would find Albert and ask him some questions.

Celia and Jonathan merely replied, "Yes, ma'am."

The gardens turned out to be spacious and interesting, full of blooming flowers and green shrubs, with several streams running through them. Mandie loved the quaint, steeply curved bridges over the water. She and her friends stopped at the peak of one to glimpse the countryside from its height. Snowball sat on the stone rail.

"I see the widow's house over there," Mandie said, pointing in the direction of a stone structure. Turning to Celia she added, "You know, we ought to go visit her. I'd like to see what she looks like."

Celia smiled at Mandie and said, "She has a son, you know. I wonder what he's like."

"Too bad no one around here has a beautiful daughter," Jonathan said sarcastically.

"Oh, but the miller has a daughter," Mandie told him. "Remember, Albert said something about staying up until his sister came home."

"She's probably ten feet tall like her brother and her father," Jonathan said, turning away to look down into the stream below. "There're fish down there. Look."

Snowball evidently saw the fish, too. He chose that moment to jump into the stream from his high perch.

"Snowball! You could drown!" Mandie shouted as the kitten splashed into the water. She quickly ran down the bridge to call him from the side of the stream.

Snowball didn't seem to be hurt. He was paddling in the water trying to catch the fish. Mandie tried to coax him to the shore.

Mrs. Taft and Senator Morton were sitting on a bench nearby and had seen the cat leap into the water. They came hurrying over to see if he was all right.

"Is he all right, Amanda?" Mrs. Taft asked.

"Yes, Grandmother. He's just wild about fish," Mandie explained as she stooped to reach out and catch him.

Snowball still had his leash on, and Mandie managed to grasp the end that floated in the water. She began pulling on it, and although the white kitten didn't want to leave the water, she managed to get him out. He immediately shook all over to get the water off his fur, and everyone had to stand back to keep from getting wet.

"Snowball, this is it. You are going up to our room and staying there for the night," Mandie declared, pulling firmly on the leash to guide him up the pathway.

"Don't pick him up, dear, or you'll ruin your dress. When you get him into the house, try to dry him off with a towel," Mrs. Taft told her. "The rest of us will wait for you in the parlor, as I suspect it's about time we had our tea."

"Yes, Grandmother," Mandie replied as Snowball suddenly began running ahead and she had to hold on to his leash more firmly.

By the time they reached the house the kitten was almost dry. He stopped at the doorway to wash himself with his tongue. Celia went upstairs with Mandie to their room while everyone else headed for the parlor.

The girls met Gretchen in the upstairs hallway. The maid stopped in surprise.

"You are back so soon?" Gretchen asked.

"Yes, my cat jumped into the stream from one of the bridges in the garden," Mandie explained. "He was after the fish. He is always running away or getting into some kind of mischief. In fact, the first night we were here someone left our door open while we were out, and he got out and turned up in my grandmother's room."

"Oh, dear, dear. It must have been Anna," Gretchen said, clucking her tongue. "I told her, in sign language of course, not to go into your room because of the cat. She must not have understood. I am sorry."

"Also, someone had locked all the doors after we went out, and when we came back Jonathan had to go up on the roof and go through our window to come down and let us in. Come to think of it, Anna came out the front door before he got down to it," Mandie said.

"Yes, that was Anna, too. She cannot hear, so she locks everything up. If someone comes in unexpectedly, she will not hear them," Gretchen explained. "She is used to the van Courtlands always keeping the doors locked also."

"Well, I'm glad to know who did these things," Mandie said.

"We looked everywhere for Snowball that night, and we found a room behind the flower room. It was dark, but we saw someone in bed," Celia put in.

"That is Anna's room. Most likely Anna was the person you saw," Gretchen said. "Now, if you are back from your walk, then Mrs. Taft is also back and she will be wanting tea."

Mandie smiled and said, "You're right. She and Senator Morton and Jonathan are in the parlor, and we'll be down as soon as I take care of Snowball."

"Yes, I will prepare the tea," Gretchen said, hurrying on down the hallway.

The girls went on to their room, and Mandie hastily dried Snowball with a towel and then put him in the bathroom.

"He's still a little wet, and I don't want him getting on the bed and messing it up," Mandie said, closing the bathroom door. "Well, I'm glad Gretchen could at least explain some of the mysterious happenings around here, aren't you?"

"Yes, and I wonder what she would know about other things, like who it was we saw in the field that night, and who changed the position of the windmill blades," Celia said as she quickly ran a brush through her long auburn curls.

"I doubt that she would know about any of that," Mandie said as she also brushed back her blonde hair. "I hope tea doesn't take long, so we can go back over to the miller's house."

"There still may not be anyone at home," Celia said as the girls went into the hallway.

"We won't know until we go see," Mandie said as they walked on downstairs to the parlor.

Tea didn't take long because Senator Morton said he must get up to his room and write some letters. And Mrs. Taft then decided she would retire for the night.

"I know it's still rather early, so you young people may stay down here for a while, but I am going to my rooms to relax. Don't stay up too late," Mrs. Taft told them as she left the parlor.

"Yes, ma'am," the three chorused as they looked at one another and smiled. As soon as Mrs. Taft had gone up the stairs Mandie rose and asked, "Is anyone coming with me? I'm going back to the miller's house."

Jonathan and Celia also stood.

"I'm not sure what you girls are up to, but since it's dark outside now, I'll go along with you," Jonathan offered.

"Suit yourself," Mandie said as she started for the door.

"I'm coming, too," Celia said.

Mandie led the way again through the flower fields and over the far bridge that spanned the canal to the miller's house. It was dark, but the moon was shining and they could see the windmill blades in the distance. They were still set to show that the mill was closed.

"Mr. Van Dongen must have had the mill closed all day," Mandie said as they walked into the yard of the miller's house. "And I can't see the sign of a light at all in the house." She hurried on up to the front door and began knocking loudly.

Jonathan and Celia stood by waiting and listening for any hint of someone around. Everything was quiet except for the noise Mandie made knocking on the door.

Finally she gave up and turned to her friends. "Evidently there's no one at home. Let's try the windmill again."

The three hastily ran to the windmill and examined the door. "It's locked," Mandie said with a big sigh. She beat on it furiously in her disappointment, and then turned to lean back against the door frame.

"I suppose we'd better go back to the house, so we won't be so late getting in, Mandie," Celia told her.

"They've probably gone away for a day or two," Jonathan remarked.

"Since not even the maid is around, she either works days or only a few hours," Mandie decided. She rubbed her knuckles. They were sore from pounding on the locked door.

Jonathan and Celia stood silently as a hush fell over the night air.

Suddenly Mandie caught a slight sound coming from somewhere. "Listen!" she whispered to her friends. The three froze in silence. The sound came again.

"It sounds like a moan to me," Mandie whispered as she softly turned to try to figure out where it was coming from.

Then a louder sound came from inside the windmill. The three leaned hard on the door, but it was still locked.

"There's someone inside!" Mandie whispered hoarsely.

"Let's look for a window," Jonathan suggested as he hurried around the structure to examine the walls. Mandie and Celia followed.

"You know, it could be that big cat," Celia guessed.

Mandie stopped and looked at her. "You may be right. Albert said the cat stays in the mill to keep out the rats." She went back to the door and called through the keyhole, "Kitty, kitty, kitty!"

"That cat probably doesn't know what *kitty* means," Jonathan said. But at that moment a loud meow came from inside the windmill.

"Oh, shucks!" Mandie said with a sigh. "We might as well go."

She lifted her long skirts and raced back across the flower fields to the bridge over the canal and on to the house, with Celia and Jonathan close behind. She thought about the Van Dongens not being home and an uneasy feeling hit her in the stomach. Something was wrong, she felt sure of it. Tomorrow she would check on them again.

Chapter 9 / Investigation in the Darkness

After reaching the house where they were staying, the three young people sat on the stairway and made plans for an early morning visit to the miller's house.

"Before breakfast," Mandie told her friends. "We'll be back in time to eat."

"All right, I'll go along with that," Jonathan told her.

"And I'll see that we get up real early so we have plenty of time," Celia volunteered.

"I just know something is wrong over there," Mandie said, pushing back her tousled hair. "Mr. Van Dongen and Albert both acted strange when we tried to find out about the position of the windmill blades and the person we saw in the dark. I have an idea they have gone away somewhere until we leave here on our journey, so we can't bother them anymore with questions."

"But, Mandie, the cat is in the mill. We heard it," Celia insisted.

"That doesn't mean anything. They could have put out enough food for it to last a few days," Mandie said.

"Or they figured it could live off the rats in the flour mill until they returned," Jonathan added with his mischievous grin.

Mandie was still suspicious of Jonathan concerning the mixing of the blue and yellow paint in the Delftware factory, and she wouldn't let herself smile at his remark.

"What time should we get up?" Celia asked.

"Let's go before daylight. That way no one will see us," Mandie told her. "I'm not sure what time it gets light here in Holland, but I think if we met right here about four-thirty or five o'clock it would still be dark."

Jonathan and Celia nodded their agreement, and the three went to their rooms to sleep until then.

When the girls got to their room, they were greeted by loud howls from Snowball shut up in the bathroom.

"It's a wonder he doesn't wake up everybody in the house," Mandie said as she hurried to open the bathroom door. Snowball came out so fast, Mandie almost tripped over him.

"What's wrong with him?" Celia asked as the cat jumped up on the bed.

"It's past his bedtime and he thinks he has to sleep in the bed," Mandie said with a little laugh.

She watched while the white kitten quickly washed his face as he sat in the middle of the bed and then circled round and round before he finally curled up in the center of it.

"At least he has sense enough to go to bed when it's time to go to bed," Celia said with a big yawn as she unbuttoned the back of her dress.

"I'll have to shut him back up in the bathroom when we leave in the morning. I sure hope he doesn't howl and wake up everyone," Mandie said as she prepared for bed.

"It might be better if you just took him with us," Celia said.

"Maybe you're right," Mandie replied.

The girls finally got into bed and drifted off to sleep. A few hours later Mandie was awakened by Celia gently shaking her.

"It's four-thirty, Mandie," Celia whispered as she stepped down from the high bed.

Mandie rubbed her eyes and jumped out of bed. Snowball tumbled out behind her and sat on the carpet in surprise.

"We have to hurry and wake Jonathan," Mandie said softly as she quickly pulled on a dress and stepped into her shoes. She parted the curtain to peek outside. It was still dark.

Celia was dressed by the time Mandie was ready, but when they started to leave, Snowball suddenly set up a howl.

"Oh, hush!" Mandie said, stooping to pick him up and shake him gently. "You must stay here and be quiet." She hurried across the room, pushed him into the bathroom, and closed the door. That made him howl all the louder. Opening the door again, Mandie gave him a little pat and said, "Snowball, stop that!"

But the white kitten would not be consoled.

"Mandie, why don't we just take him with us? I'll help you tend to him," Celia said.

"I suppose we'll have to," Mandie said, gathering his leash and carrying the kitten into the hallway. He immediately tried to lick his mistress' face. "Let's go. I'll carry him until we get outside."

The girls quietly knocked on Jonathan's door, and he immediately opened it and slipped outside into the hallway. Not daring to speak a word for fear of being heard by someone in the house, the three quickly went down the stairs and outside.

"Let's hurry," Mandie spoke at last as they started across the flower field. She still carried Snowball in her arms, because it was faster that way.

Jonathan and Celia stayed right behind Mandie, and they soon arrived at the miller's house. As soon as she could see the windmill blades in the darkness, Mandie noticed that they were still in the closed position. Mr. Van Dongen was probably not home, she decided in disappointment as she hurried up to the door of the house. It didn't occur to her until that moment that it was an odd time to go knocking on someone's door. If he was at home and came to answer her knock, what in this world would she say to him? She was sure he'd really be angry this time. She paused, her hand in the air.

"Well, aren't you going to knock on the door?" Jonathan whispered behind her.

Mandie quickly turned and motioned for her friends to move away from the house. She stopped near the flower gardens.

"Well, what now?" Jonathan asked in a soft voice.

"I don't think we ought to go knocking on Mr. Van Dongen's door this early in the morning. He might not like it," Mandie began. "And if he—"

Jonathan interrupted, "You mean we went to all this trouble for nothing? You're afraid to knock on the door?"

"Sh-h-h!" Mandie cautioned him. "We don't have to knock. We can just walk around the house and look in all the windows."

"But it's dark in there, Mandie," Celia reminded her.

"If you're afraid to knock, I'll go and knock," Jonathan said, quickly rushing back to the front door of the house.

Without waiting for the girls, he began knocking loudly, the sound reverberating in the silent morning air.

Mandie and Celia waited by the flower garden to see what would happen. After a few minutes, without any response, Jonathan walked back to rejoin the girls.

"No one is home," he remarked flatly.

"I'm sure they would have heard you if there had been anyone in the house," Mandie told him. "I'm going to the windmill and see if I can still hear the cat inside." She hurried toward the huge structure as she held Snowball tightly in her arms. Celia and Jonathan followed.

Mandie tried the door. It was still locked. The three of them walked around the mill, but saw no one anywhere. They stopped by the door again and listened for the cat.

After a few moments Mandie said, "I can't hear a thing." Snowball squirmed in her arms to get down. "Snowball, stop it. I know you just want to run away."

At that moment there was the faint sound of the cat inside, and Snowball struggled futilely to escape from Mandie's arms.

"Snowball hears the other cat," Celia whispered.

Then there was a thumping noise inside the mill. The three young people looked at one another in the pale darkness. At that moment, Mandie relaxed her grasp on the kitten and he managed to jump out of her arms. He raced around the mill, Mandie chasing after him.

"Snowball, come here!" Mandie called.

The white kitten didn't respond, and when he glimpsed the lower blade of the windmill, he leaped into the air and landed on the metal network far above Mandie's reach.

Mandie stomped her foot as she stood there helplessly looking up at her cat. Snowball meowed, and then began making his way on up the blade.

"That crazy cat!" Mandie exclaimed in exasperation. "Look at him!"

"Looks like he's headed for that window up there," Jonathan remarked.

"We'll never get him down," Celia said with a sigh.

Snowball continued to climb, and Mandie decided he would indeed reach the window if he didn't change direction.

"Snowball!" Mandie called out to him. "Come back down here!"

The kitten turned to look down at his mistress, loudly meowed, and then jumped over onto the ledge of the high window. He sniffed around the opening and then sat down on the narrow frame, meowing loudly again at his mistress below.

"How will we ever get him down?" Celia fussed.

"He got himself up there, let him get down the same way," Jonathan said in a disgusted tone.

Mandie was worried about her kitten, and still angry with Jonathan about the paint incident. She decided she would have to go up and get Snowball herself. Without even thinking about the height or the danger, she jumped up and managed to catch the edge of the blade. Hanging on with all her might, she worked her way up until she had her feet on the metal network.

"Mandie, please don't climb any higher," Celia begged.

"You'll fall and break every bone," Jonathan warned. "I'll come up and help you." He started to grasp the end of the lower blade.

"No!" Mandie called down to him. "This may not be strong enough to hold both of us. I'll go myself."

She wiggled around and managed to move up another few inches. Suddenly the blade began moving. She tightened her grasp to keep from falling and the blade stopped. She tried to move up farther, and found her full skirt was caught on the metal work. Holding on with one hand, she tried to pull her skirt free, but every time she looked down her head began to swim.

Celia waved and called up to her, "Our verse, Mandie, remember our verse!"

Through the loud roar of panic in her head, Mandie heard her friend but couldn't open her mouth to utter one word.

Celia tried again, "Mandie, 'What time I am afraid I will put my trust in Thee.' Can you say it, Mandie?"

"I'll go get help," Jonathan muttered.

"No, I'll go," Celia said quickly. "You stay here. You might be able to help her in some way because you're stronger than I am." She called, "Mandie, I'll go back to the house and bring someone to help. Hang on!" She lifted her long skirt and raced off through the flower fields.

Mandie tried to see Jonathan below, but she couldn't move very far because her skirt held her captive. She looked up at Snowball, who was still meowing loudly, and her blue eyes traveled on to the lightening sky. She gazed at the streaks of daylight above and finally found her voice. "What time I am afraid I will put my trust in Thee," she quoted her favorite Bible verse. "Please help me, dear God," she prayed. Then she closed her eyes and tightened her grasp on the rough metal network. Somehow she would get back down, but she wished she could think of a way to save her precious kitten. Suddenly, Mandie felt a calm come over her and she was able to think again.

"Mandie, let me try coming up to help you," Jonathan called from below.

"No, I don't think this thing would hold us both. Besides, the blade has moved up higher, and I don't think you could reach it," Mandie told him.

"Well, for goodness sake, hold on for all you're worth, then," Jonathan replied.

Mandie felt as though she had been hanging on for hours when Celia returned, but, in fact, it had been only a matter of minutes. The sound of horse's hooves reached Mandie's ears, and she strained her neck to see who was coming. Then she heard a low bird whistle, and tears of joy ran down her cheeks. It was Uncle Ned. Her father's dear old Cherokee friend, who had promised to watch over Mandie when Jim Shaw died, was always nearby to fulfill his vow.

"Uncle Ned!" Mandie cried out to him as she heard the horse stop below.

"Papoose, hold tight!" Uncle Ned called up to her as he quickly dismounted and looked around.

"Her skirt is caught. She can't move up or down," Celia told the old Indian.

"Take off skirt, Papoose," Uncle Ned told Mandie without hesitation.

"Take off my skirt? I can't, Uncle Ned. It's stuck," Mandie said as she finally managed to get a slight glimpse of him.

"Yes, you can, Mandie," Celia told her. "You have on a skirt and waist. All you have to do is unbutton the waistband and let the skirt fall."

Mandie thought about that for a second and said, "I'll try."

"Hold tight with one hand," Uncle Ned cautioned her. "Unbutton skirt with other. Careful."

Mandie slowly released one hand and immediately felt her weight pull on the other hand. She grasped the metal again and then tried moving one hand once more to her skirt. With stiff fingers she finally found the button, and gritting her teeth and holding her breath she pulled until she felt the band come apart and the long heavy skirt began sliding down. She quickly grasped the metal again with both hands.

"Papoose, move up a bit. Must get out of skirt," Uncle Ned directed. "Careful."

Mandie took a deep breath and did as he told her. She managed to slide up out of the skirt, and it fell away and hung on the blade. Fortunately, her petticoat was not caught. She was free. She would go after Snowball. She couldn't leave him up there.

"Now, Papoose, come down to end of blade. I catch Papoose," the old Indian told her.

"I can't, Uncle Ned. I've got to get Snowball," Mandie wailed.

"No. Papoose come down. I get Snowball," Uncle Ned said firmly. "Come down, Papoose."

She trusted Uncle Ned. He would get Snowball down for her. She glanced up at the white kitten who was crying loudly.

"Just wait, Snowball," she called to him, and then began slowly working her way down the metal network of the blade.

"Slow, Papoose," Uncle Ned spoke again to her.

Mandie finally reached the end of the blade but found that she was much higher in the air than before because the blade had moved upward. It was too far to swing off onto the ground.

Uncle Ned also realized she was too high for him to reach her. "Stop, Papoose. Hold tight," he told her.

He quickly brought his horse beneath the end of the blade, and then jumping onto the horse's back he stood straight up and easily reached the frightened girl.

Mandie's tears wet the shoulder of Uncle Ned's deerskin jacket as he held her tight and stepped down to the ground.

Mandie still clung to him and said in a trembling voice, "Oh, Uncle Ned, I'm always so glad to see you, but I think this morning I was more glad than ever."

Uncle Ned squeezed her tight and then helped her to sit on a log. Celia stooped to put an arm around her, while Jonathan nervously kicked the sand nearby.

"Papoose, sit here. I go after white kitten now," Uncle Ned told her.

Mandie watched as once again the old Indian climbed onto his horse's back. He reached the end of the windmill blade easily, and quickly worked his way up to where Snowball was making such a fuss. At first the kitten backed away, but Uncle Ned managed to pick him up by the scruff of his neck and set him on his shoulder. The kitten clung to the deerskin jacket as the old Indian made his way down. Mandie jumped up to catch him as Uncle Ned passed the kitten down to her.

"Now we go," Uncle Ned announced as he stepped to the ground.

Mandie suddenly remembered she was only wearing her heavy white petticoat. She gasped and said, "Uncle Ned, my skirt is still hanging on the blade."

As they all looked upward, the blades began moving slowly until the one with the skirt hanging on it was high above the others.

"Who move the blade?" Uncle Ned asked. "Miller is here?"

"No, Uncle Ned, we haven't seen him—" Mandie began.

"I told you why we were here, Uncle Ned," Celia reminded him.

"Yes, to find miller," the old Indian replied. "But someone move blades. Not move alone."

"You're right," Mandie agreed. "The blades are supposed to be locked into position, and they couldn't just move like that."

"Not unless there's something wrong with the mechanism," Jonathan added.

"We find what make blades move," Uncle Ned decided as he walked around looking for the door.

"It's this way," Jonathan said, leading them around the structure.

As they rounded the building toward the door, Mandie heard someone running. She raced ahead to see who it was, but only saw the bushes move in the field, and then looked back to find the door standing open—the same door that had been locked earlier.

"There was someone here!" she exclaimed, holding on to Snowball.

"And whoever it was ran away," Jonathan added.

Uncle Ned moved through the doorway and Mandie and her friends followed. The sun was coming up now and lighted the interior of the mill. Mandie heard a slight meow from the corner, and the big gray cat came bounding out and through the door. She had to secure Snowball tightly to keep him from following.

As they moved farther into the mill, Mandie spotted someone lying in the corner on the floor. She stepped forward and bent for a better look. "It's Mr. Van Dongen!" Mandie exclaimed.

The others crowded around as Uncle Ned stooped to examine the man. His hands and feet were tied up and there was a gag in his mouth, but he seemed to be awake. When Uncle Ned was near enough for the man to see him, he attempted to yell through the gag. The old Indian quickly took a knife from his pocket and cut the ropes that bound his wrists and ankles. Then he removed the gag.

"Mr. Van Dongen, are you all right?" Mandie asked anxiously, bending over the miller as Uncle Ned helped him sit up.

"Water," the man managed to say.

"There's a pump outside," Mandie said to Jonathan.

"I'll get some," the boy volunteered.

Mr. Van Dongen was trying to get the circulation back into his hands and feet, and Uncle Ned helped massage them.

Jonathan rushed back in with a pail of water and a dipper and hurried to give the man a drink of water. Mr. Van Dongen drank some of it, and then poured the rest over his face, all the while keeping his eyes on Uncle Ned.

Mandie and Celia stooped nearby, and Mandie asked, "Mr. Van Dongen, who did this to you?"

The man looked at Mandie, puzzled, and she remembered that she was in her petticoat. She straightened it self-consciously.

"It was all a misunderstanding," Mr. Van Dongen said, trying to get to his feet.

Uncle Ned helped to steady him, and the miller finally asked, "You are a real American Indian?"

"Cherokee, sir," Uncle Ned said. "Friend of Jim Shaw, father of Papoose," he said, nodding at Mandie. "We walk now," he urged the man.

Mr. Van Dongen looked again at Mandie, and then allowed Uncle Ned to escort him from the mill.

"How long have you been in here, Mr. Van Dongen?" Jonathan asked.

"Long enough to know better next time," the Dutchman replied.

"Mr. Van Dongen, we heard someone run away when

we came to the door," Celia told him.

"Yes, and the door was open. It was locked before I got caught on the windmill blade," Mandie said.

"Caught on the windmill blade?" the miller asked, hobbling forward.

Mandie explained. "When I started up after Snowball, someone moved the blade and my skirt got caught. I hope you don't mind. It's still hanging up there."

"Go home now," Mr. Van Dongen said. "We'll worry about the skirt and this whole incident tomorrow." He shook his head. "You had better go get another skirt on before your grandmother catches you."

His remark brought a laugh from all three young people.

"But, Mr. Van Dongen, you never did tell us what happened," Mandie insisted.

"We've been checking to see if you were home. We were worried about you. Have you been in the mill all this time?" Jonathan asked.

The Dutchman took a key from his pocket, unlocked the door to his house, and said, "Good-night. It may be morning, but I intend to get a good night's sleep. Good day." He stepped inside and closed the door.

"We go now," Uncle Ned said simply.

"When did you get here, Uncle Ned?" Mandie asked. "I've been waiting for you to arrive."

"Late last night," the old Indian said.

"He was up early, and was in the yard when I went back to the house for help," Celia explained.

"I'm so glad you came when you did," Mandie said, reaching to squeeze the old man's hand. "Thank you."

"Papoose must learn to think," Uncle Ned repeated his familiar advice. "Think before doing."

"I know it's kind of late, but I'm doing a lot of thinking

right now, Uncle Ned," Mandie told him. "Things could have been really awful if you hadn't arrived. And I'm also thinking about Mr. Van Dongen. He didn't want to talk to us about whatever happened to him, and I wonder why."

"And who was it that ran away from the door to the mill?" Jonathan wondered aloud.

"We'll eventually find all the answers," Mandie assured him, giving Uncle Ned a big smile.

Chapter 10 / Where Did Everybody Go?

Back at the house, Mandie barely got into her room before Mrs. Taft, on her way downstairs, tapped on the girls' door and called to them, "Amanda, Celia, time for breakfast."

Mandie dropped Snowball onto the carpet and ran into the bathroom. Celia opened their door slightly and smiled at Mrs. Taft. "Yes, ma'am, we'll be right down."

Mrs. Taft kept going, and Celia quickly closed the door.

"Mandie, please hurry," Celia called to her through the bathroom door.

Mandie cleaned up and put on fresh clothes while Celia changed hers. Snowball washed himself methodically on the carpet.

"I'm so glad Uncle Ned is finally here," Mandie said as she pulled on clean stockings. "We need his help to solve some of this mystery."

"I hope somebody can figure out what's going on,"

Celia replied. She brushed out her long auburn hair.

"There is something that Mr. Van Dongen doesn't want to tell us," Mandie said. Turning to look at her friend she added, "Come to think of it, I wonder where Albert is? He must be gone somewhere or he would have found his father!"

"Of course," Celia agreed, tying a green ribbon in her hair to match her dress.

"Mr. Van Dongen must have some enemies who tied him up like that. Why, he could have died in there, starved to death or something, if we hadn't found him," Mandie said, shaking out her long skirt.

"I'm about to starve to death, Mandie. Let's go," Celia urged her friend.

Mandie looked down at Snowball curled up on the rug asleep. "I'll have to take him or he won't get anything to eat." She reached down and scooped him up in her arms.

Gretchen met the girls at the door to the parlor and took the kitten to the kitchen.

Mrs. Taft, Senator Morton, Uncle Ned, and Jonathan were already sitting at the table. The girls exchanged greetings with the adults, and Mandie sat down next to Uncle Ned, with Celia on her other side next to Jonathan.

"We had to wait breakfast for you," Mrs. Taft said, looking sternly at Mandie and Celia.

"I'm sorry, Grandmother," Mandie said with a faint smile.

"I apologize, Mrs. Taft," Celia told her.

Mandie looked at Jonathan and whispered, "How did you get here so fast?"

"It doesn't take boys as long to dress as girls, with all their frills and long hair," Jonathan said with his mischievous grin.

"Oh, I know how fast you move," Mandie replied briskly. "It didn't take you long to mix that paint at the factory!"

Uncle Ned heard the exchange and frowned. "Think, Papoose, think before you speak, before you act."

"Yes, Uncle Ned," Mandie replied in a whisper. "But you don't know what happened at the factory. I'll tell you as soon as I get a chance."

Uncle Ned looked at Mandie with a puzzled expression.

Mrs. Taft spoke across the table to Uncle Ned. "I'm so glad you have arrived, sir. I know how much you enjoy being with the young people. Senator Morton and I would like to go into town to a music presentation today. Maybe you wouldn't mind keeping an eye on these three."

The old Indian smiled and said, "Be glad, madam."

The three young people exchanged glances and grinned. Mandie knew her Indian friend was not nearly as strict as her grandmother, and she was anxious to carry on with the solution to the mystery surrounding the windmill.

"When are y'all going?" Mandie asked too quickly, sipping her hot coffee.

"As soon as we finish breakfast," Mrs. Taft told her. "Now, Amanda, I expect you to inform Uncle Ned of your whereabouts at all times. Don't be causing him any trouble."

"Of course not, ma'am. We will be with Uncle Ned, or tell him where we are going," Mandie answered as respectfully as possible.

When everyone had finished with breakfast, Mrs. Taft and Senator Morton left the room to prepare for their trip into town. The young people and Uncle Ned gathered in the parlor, and Gretchen brought Mandie her cat. She tethered him to a chair on his leash.

"Uncle Ned, I'd like to talk to you for a few minutes," Mandie began. She looked at Celia, and the girl caught her wish immediately.

"Come on, Jonathan," she said, "let's go outside and walk around to where we can see the windmill. She undid Snowball's leash from the chair and said, "I'll take him out for some air, Mandie."

"Thank you," Mandie told her with a smile.

Jonathan, walking toward the door, asked, "Are you two coming outside later?"

"Of course. We'll be out in a few minutes," Mandie assured him. "Don't go off to the miller's without us."

Jonathan stopped and looked at her. "Mr. Van Dongen is probably still asleep. Remember? He said he was going to sleep."

"That's right. But we'll be out in a few minutes anyway," Mandie said.

Jonathan and Celia left the parlor, and Mandie turned on the settee to face her Cherokee friend.

"Uncle Ned, Jonathan has done an awful thing and I'm really worried about him," Mandie blurted.

"Jonathan?" the old man questioned.

"You see, we went to the Delftware factory yesterday, and they have this blue paint that they paint all the dishes with. But they also had a huge barrel of yellow paint for the walls," Mandie began. "Jonathan joked about what would happen if we mixed the blue and the yellow together, making it green, of course. Then he disappeared for a few minutes, and when he came back the worker in front of us was painting a piece of porcelain and the paint he was using from the funnel suddenly turned green!"

Uncle Ned frowned and asked, "Did Jonathan boy say he put blue and yellow paint together?"

"Oh, no, he denied it," Mandie quickly replied.

"Then Papoose think Jonathan boy lie?" Uncle Ned asked.

"He did lie, I'm sure, Uncle Ned," Mandie said.

Uncle Ned reached to take her small white hand in his old, dark, wrinkled one. "Papoose, think. Must not accuse. Even with proof. Must tell grown people. They straighten it out," he tried to explain to her.

"But I can't tell anyone, Uncle Ned. Senator Morton said the Royal family might be angry enough to hang whoever did it," Mandie said.

"Papoose ask Jonathan's forgiveness. Then forget it," Uncle Ned advised. "Papoose not know anything for sure."

"But, Uncle Ned, I feel like he did it. In fact, I don't have any proof, but I'm sure he did it," Mandie insisted as she withdrew her hand from his.

"Think, Papoose, think," he reminded her. He stood up. "Papoose go ask forgiveness now."

"But I can't, Uncle Ned. I feel so sure he did it," Mandie repeated. She looked up at him and said, "I want to tell you about the miller, too."

Uncle Ned sat down again, and Mandie related the events concerning the miller and his son. She told him about meeting the son at the inn, and then about all of them going to visit at his house. She mentioned the miller's abrupt remark that he had to go back to work, and they had to leave. She explained about the windmill blades, and also told him of the man and the girl they had seen leave the parade.

"It may not sound connected, but I believe it is," Mandie said.

"Maybe," the old Indian said. "Maybe connected to paint at factory, too."

Mandie thought about that for a minute, then decided

it couldn't be. The Delftware factory was a long way from here. "I don't see how it could be related," she said. "Anyway, we ought to go back to see the miller. Maybe he will be ready to answer some questions for us." She stood up.

"We go, but Papoose must not cause miller anger," the old man warned her.

They stepped outside, and found Celia and Jonathan on a bench in the flower garden. Snowball was anchored to the leg of the bench, but still had room to play around at the end of the long leash.

"Where are the windmill blades set?" Mandie asked as she approached them.

"They're set in the position to show that the mill is closed, just like they've been so far," Jonathan answered.

"Well, I suppose we can't go over there until the miller gets his nap," Mandie said. "Why don't we show Uncle Ned around the house?"

"That's a good idea," Celia said, rising from the bench.

"Wait, I know a better idea," Mandie said. "We've been wanting to go see the widow's house. Let's all walk over that way."

"Why not? We may even meet up with her son," Jonathan teased.

Mandie looked straight at him and said, "Maybe we will." She saw Uncle Ned looking at her. She turned to Celia and said, "Let's go. I'll take Snowball." Celia untied the leash from the bench, and Mandie secured it firmly, although Snowball attempted to make a dash for it.

Mandie led the way to the road. As they neared the house, Mandie realized it was larger than she had first thought. It was surrounded by flower gardens, and weeping willows lined the walk from the road.

They all paused at the walkway.

"Should we go up and knock on the door?" Celia asked.

"I'll knock on the door," Mandie said, going ahead down the lane.

"What are you going to say when someone comes to the door?" Jonathan asked as he quickened his steps.

Mandie stopped and looked at him. "I'll just tell whoever it is that we've come to visit," she said.

"That might not go over too well," Jonathan whispered as he looked back at Uncle Ned who followed at a brief distance. "I mean, with a real live Indian with us."

Mandie stopped, put her hands on her hips, and said, "Jonathan Guyer! Do you forget I'm one-fourth Cherokee?"

"Of course not, Mandie, but these people in Europe don't have people like him living around them. They've probably never seen an American Indian," Jonathan quickly whispered back.

"Well, they're going to see one now," Mandie said, holding on to Snowball's leash and marching up to the front door. Lifting the knocker she banged it several times.

The others stood by waiting and listening. There was no response.

"Must not be anyone home," Celia said.

"Let's go to the back," Mandie suggested, leading the way to the back door. She quickly knocked again. No one came. The house was silent.

"Papoose, people not home," Uncle Ned finally spoke up.

"Well, I guess you're right," Mandie admitted reluctantly. "Seems like we can never find anyone at home. Let's go back, and we'll show you the house, Uncle Ned. It has lots of nooks and crannies."

Back at the house, Mandie began upstairs and showed Uncle Ned each room, having familiarized herself with them on their search for Snowball their first night there. However, since it was daytime, the young people had a chance to see everything better than they had that night. The furniture seemed to be mostly antiques, and everything was clean and in order.

After looking in all the rooms upstairs Mandie remarked, "None of these rooms look occupied. Where do you suppose Gretchen sleeps?"

"She may be a day maid, Mandie," Celia told her.

"But she is here so much I believe she must live here." Changing the subject, Mandie said, "Remember the locked door we found in that small bedroom that seemed to lead to the attic?"

"Yes," Jonathan said. "Did you want to check it again?"

"Lets," Mandie answered.

When they found the room and tried the inside door, they discovered that it was still locked.

"Why would they keep a door to the attic locked? Not only that, this door looks like all the other doors to the rooms up here," Mandie said.

"One door, Papoose miss," Uncle Ned said with a twinkle in his eye.

"Where, Uncle Ned, where?" Mandie asked.

"Room with books," he replied, pointing.

"Show us, Uncle Ned," Mandie said.

The old Indian led them down the hallway and around the turn to a small room that was evidently a sitting room for the huge bedroom next to it. He walked across the carpet and motioned toward a panel in the wall. "There," he said. The wall was in the shadow of bookshelves and freestanding screens.

Celia and Jonathan crowded close, and Mandie examined the panel. Uncle Ned was right. There was a small handle ring almost concealed in the wood. She turned the handle and pulled. It didn't budge. Then she tried pushing, and it opened up onto a narrow staircase.

"Uncle Ned, you are a detective!" Mandie exclaimed as she began to climb the stairs. She handed the end of Snowball's leash to Celia. "I'm going up. Anybody want to join me?" Without waiting for an answer, she started up.

"Papoose, be careful," Uncle Ned warned.

"I'll be careful, Uncle Ned," she promised as she slowly ascended the steps.

Jonathan followed, but Celia stayed back with Uncle Ned.

Arriving at the top of the stairs, Mandie could see a little more clearly, and she found a door. She tried it, but it was locked.

"It's locked, of course," she called down.

Jonathan tried it, too, but it wouldn't budge. He and Mandie went down the way they'd come without exchanging a word.

"Let's show Uncle Ned the downstairs and that flower room," Mandie suggested, leading the way to the first floor. She took Snowball's leash from Celia.

Finally locating the room full of flowers, Mandie turned to Uncle Ned. "Do you see anything here that grows back home, or is it all Dutch?"

Uncle Ned examined the plants and flowers. Every inch of table, chairs, and shelves was covered with something growing in pots of every size.

Mandie watched as Uncle Ned finally shook his head and said, "None of these in America." He surveyed the room, and came to the door the young people had found that night.

"That's Anna's room, I think," Mandie said. She rapped lightly on the door, and then remembered that Anna was deaf. "You know, we haven't seen a single servant since breakfast. I wonder where they all went? Maybe it's time for dinner."

"My stomach feels like it's time," Jonathan remarked.

"Mine, too," Celia added.

"Then we eat," Uncle Ned said.

"This way to the dining room," Mandie said, entering the hallway. She hurried ahead and pushed open the door. The table was elegantly set with china and silver, and the food was already on the table. "It's ready," Mandie said to the others.

They began to take their places, but something was wrong. Usually Gretchen called them in, and then brought the hot food. Now the food was laid out and getting cold.

"Where is everybody?" Mandie asked. She tied Snowball's leash to a chair leg.

"Let me look in the kitchen to see if Gretchen or Anna is there," Mandie said as she hurried out of the dining room.

She found no one, but the fire was going in the cookstove and there was a steaming pot of coffee ready to serve. She couldn't understand what was going on.

Hurrying back to the dining room she said, "Wait just one more minute. I'm going to run to the barn."

She hurried out the back door and down the pathway to the barn. After checking each room and stall, she couldn't find anyone there, either. Even the van Courtland's cart and horse were gone, and of course William had taken their rented carriage to drive Mrs. Taft and Senator Morton into town. Something strange was happening.

When she got back to the dining room, her friends had taken seats and were waiting for her. She pulled out a chair by Uncle Ned and sat down.

"There is nobody anywhere. It seems strange to me," Mandie said, catching her breath after the fast trip to the barn.

"Food hot. People not gone long," Uncle Ned said as he picked up a bowl of steaming potatoes.

"You're right, Uncle Ned. Anna must have cooked the food, and Gretchen set it out for us. Then they must have had to leave in a hurry for some reason," Mandie remarked, helping herself to a roll. "Oh, there's coffee on the stove. I'll get it." She started to push back her chair, but Uncle Ned stopped her.

"I get hot coffee," he said. He got up and went to the kitchen. In a moment he returned with the pot and filled their cups with the dark, aromatic liquid.

"Do you suppose someone got sick, or hurt, and had to rush to the doctor or something?" Celia asked as she filled her plate.

"Maybe," Jonathan said, taking some of everything.

"We thank big God for food," Uncle Ned announced.

The young people laid down their forks and waited for the old Indian to return thanks. "We thank you, Mighty Father, for this food, for every blessing, Amen."

Mandie filled a saucer with bits of food and set it under the table for Snowball. As soon as the others had begun eating, she said, "Maybe we could go over to the miller's when we finish. He certainly ought to be up and around by now."

The others nodded, none of them looking as excited about the prospect as Mandie.

"I hope we can at least find him this time," Mandie said. "Everybody else has plumb disappeared."

At that moment there was a loud knocking at the back door.

"Apparently not everybody," Jonathan observed, pushing back his chair. "I'll see who it is."

"Well, it's about time somebody showed up," Mandie remarked as they all stopped to listen.

Mandie could hear a man speaking English with a foreign accent. "Is lady here?" the man asked.

"What lady?" Jonathan answered.

"Young lady from mill," the man tried to explain.

"Oh, you mean the miller's daughter. No, she's not here. As far as I know she lives with her father, the miller. Did you try there?" Jonathan asked the man.

"Yes. Not there. Good day," the man said.

Mandie heard Jonathan close the door, and he came back into the dining room and sat down. "I'm pretty sure that was the Chinese man we saw at the Delftware factory. He was looking for the miller's daughter."

"I wonder what he wanted with her, and why he came here looking for her?" Mandie said.

"This house next door. Girl might visit here," Uncle Ned said.

"You may be right about that, but what on earth would that Chinese man want with the miller's daughter?" Mandie asked, puzzled by the man's appearance. "Well, I guess it only adds to our mystery," she said. "Let's hurry and finish so we can try to figure out what's going on before something else happens."

The rest of the meal was eaten in silence, but Jonathan had a smile on his face.

Chapter 11 / Some Things Explained

As soon as the meal was finished, Mandie and her friends walked over to the miller's house. Mandie carried Snowball in her arms just in case they came near the Van Dongens' cat. And when they got close enough to see, Mandie noticed her skirt was no longer hanging on the windmill blade. The miller must have taken it down.

"The blades are still set for closing," Jonathan remarked as they walked along.

Mandie looked up at Uncle Ned and asked, "Do you know about the signals given by the windmill blades, Uncle Ned?"

"Yes, Papoose," the old Indian replied. "Blades good for messages. But not ladder to climb," he said seriously.

Mandie knew what he meant, and said, "I won't ever do that again, Uncle Ned. Did you notice my skirt is gone? The miller must have pulled it down."

"Yes. Must move blades to remove skirt. Now, same position as before," Uncle Ned observed.

The young people stopped to look at him. "You're right, Uncle Ned, someone had to move the blades to get the skirt," Jonathan said.

"The miller must be finished with his nap," Mandie said. "Maybe we can get him to come to the door this time."

When they came into the yard of the miller's house, Mandie went straight to the door and began knocking. Snowball pulled at the end of his leash trying to get loose.

Everyone waited and listened, but there was no response. Mandie continued knocking, and called, "Mr. Van Dongen! Mr. Van Dongen!"

Still, there was no answer.

"Let's go to the mill. Maybe he's out there," Mandie said, turning to walk toward the structure. She stopped for a moment and picked up Snowball.

As they stepped up to the door of the mill, Mandie was almost knocked down by two Chinese men who came rushing out. She dropped Snowball and he ran into the mill.

Jonathan and Uncle Ned turned to chase the two men, but they disappeared quickly into the tall bushes and trees surrounding the property.

Mandie heard her cat running around inside the mill. Evidently Snowball had found the miller's cat. "Snowball!" she called as she ran inside looking for him. Celia followed.

Even though it was daytime and the sun was shining, sections of the mill were dark. Mandie glanced around. Someone had hung pieces of heavy cloth over the windows. She walked over to uncover one window when she stumbled over something and fell onto the floor. Looking up, she discovered the miller, once again tied up and gagged.

"Mr. Van Dongen!" she cried, "Uncle Ned!"

Jonathan and Uncle Ned had just entered the mill.

Uncle Ned saw at once what Mandie was calling him for, and quickly pulled out his knife to cut the cords and set the man free.

Mr. Van Dongen, finally able to talk, said with a deep breath, "Thank you. Thank you."

"What happened, Mr. Van Dongen?" Mandie asked. "You must tell us what happened this time."

Uncle Ned helped him to his feet. "Thank you, sir," the miller said again.

The old Indian nodded.

"We saw two Chinese men run out of here," Mandie told the man. "What is going on?"

"First, my apologies to you Americans," he said, sitting down on a stool, and offering similar seats to the others. "This can no longer be a secret. I work for our government. I was told foreigners visiting our country had been causing trouble with the paint at the Delftware factory, and that all foreigners present then were suspect and being investigated."

"Oh!" Mandie held her breath and glanced at Jonathan. Was Mr. Van Dongen suspicious of the boy? Jonathan seemed interested in what the man was saying, and didn't look the least bit worried.

"I arranged with your driver to take you people to the inn where you would meet my son, and he would bring you here so I could evaluate things for myself," the miller continued.

The young people looked at one another, and Mandie noticed that Uncle Ned was leaning forward, listening to every word.

"Is that why you were so friendly to us?" Mandie asked.

Mr. Van Dongen smiled and said, "No, miss, I simply found you people interesting."

"But then you suddenly decided you had to go to work, and practically told us to leave," Mandie reminded him.

"For which I apologize, miss, but I had just remembered that I was acting in the service of my country, and that must come before friendship," Mr. Van Dongen explained.

"Where is Albert, sir? Why wasn't he here to help you?" Jonathan asked.

"Albert is away on business," the miller replied.

Uncle Ned finally joined in the conversation. "Crooks got away. Must catch them," he said.

Mandie suddenly remembered that the miller did not know Uncle Ned's name. The last time he had only said that he was a Cherokee.

"Mr. Van Dongen, this is my father's friend, Mr. Ned Sweetwater. I didn't introduce you to him last time. I call him Uncle Ned, and so does everyone else, but he's really not related to me, even though I am one-fourth Cherokee."

Mr. Van Dongen reached to shake hands. "I am pleased to meet you, sir, and I appreciate all your help."

Uncle Ned nodded, never having taken well to compliments or gratitude. He was always ready and willing to help those in need, and didn't feel their thanks was necessary.

"I don't know why we're sitting out here in the mill, when we could be in the house taking some refreshments," the miller said, rising from the stool. "We will make tea. We can close the door to the mill and leave the cats to play."

As Mandie followed, she asked, "Where is your maid, Mr. Van Dongen? We haven't seen her at all."

"She is away visiting an ailing sister," the miller explained as they stopped in front of the door to the house. He inserted his key and pushed the door open, stepping back for them to enter.

They all took seats while the miller went to brew some tea.

"Do you think anyone will catch those Chinese men, Uncle Ned?" Mandie asked, glancing at Jonathan from the corner of her eye. It had dawned on her that the Chinese men were no doubt the culprits in the paint mixing, and not Jonathan.

"Yes," the old Indian said. "They will be caught." He looked directly at Mandie. "You know, Papoose."

The others wouldn't understand what he meant by that, Mandie reasoned, but she knew that Uncle Ned was saying that she knew who was guilty, and she had better apologize to Jonathan and ask his forgiveness. She would do that as soon as the proper moment arose.

"One of those men was the same man who came to our house asking for the miller's daughter, and also the same man we saw at the Delftware factory," Jonathan revealed.

"I wonder what he wanted with Mr. Van Dongen's daughter?" Mandie asked as the miller returned to the room. She told him about the Chinese man coming to their house.

"My daughter is working odd hours," the miller said as he served the tea. "I do not know how the Chinese man could know her."

As they sat there sipping tea, Mandie heard Snowball outside meowing loudly. How did he get out of the mill?

Setting down her cup, she jumped up to go to the door. "Snowball is here. Someone let him out!"

By the time she opened the door, the men and Jonathan were right behind her. Suddenly, Mandie heard a creaking noise from the windmill. She looked up and watched as the windmill blades began to move.

Mr. Van Dongen led the way to the mill. Uncle Ned

cautioned them to be quiet. "They hear us. We not catch them."

"You are right," Mr. Van Dongen agreed. He and the old Indian quietly approached the mill. The others followed at a cautious distance.

Just as they reached the open door of the mill, the blades stopped moving. Mandie didn't understand the position at which they were set.

After Uncle Ned and Mr. Van Dongen ran inside, Mandie caught a glimpse of the Chinese men sneaking out again.

"There they are!" she called.

Uncle Ned and Mr. Van Dongen came out of the mill and raced after the men. Jonathan followed them.

"Let's stay here and watch the door," Celia suggested to Mandie.

Mandie paused. "We should. Someone needs to watch the door in case they come back."

Celia was visibly shaken by the thought, and Mandie tried to comfort her. "We won't try to capture them by ourselves."

"What if they try to capture us?" Celia asked.

Mandie frowned and said, "I don't think they'd try that. We can always run away from them." She was still holding Snowball. "Besides, Snowball will protect us. I could always throw him in their faces, and they'd leave us alone real fast."

Celia winced at the thought.

At that moment, Mandie heard the sound of distant horse's hooves. She listened as they came nearer. Pushing Celia ahead of her into the mill, she whispered, "Quick. Let's hide behind the door!"

Celia clung to Mandie, and Mandie's heartbeat quickened. She had no idea who would come riding up on a horse after all that had happened. It couldn't be the Chinese men. They were running on foot. *Could they have hidden horses somewhere?* Uncle Ned and Mr. Van Dongen had disappeared into the fields, chasing the men. Even Jonathan had gone with them.

Finally Mandie heard the horse stop outside the mill and a man called, "Whoa!" She stuck her head around the door, and relief flooded over her as she recognized Albert.

"It's Albert, Celia!" Mandie said as she hurried out into the yard.

Albert saw the girls, and before Mandie could speak he said, "This is a nice reception. Are you visiting my father?"

"We don't have time to explain, but you should take your horse and see where your father and Uncle Ned and Jonathan went," Mandie urged. "They were chasing two Chinese men into the woods. We think they are crooks."

"Chinese crooks?" Albert asked, digging his heels into the horse's sides. "Thank you. I'll be back."

The girls watched as he disappeared into the trees. Then they sat down on a nearby bench to wait for everyone to return.

"Do you know what all this means, Celia?" Mandie asked her friend as she held Snowball securely in her lap.

"Yes. The Chinese men were the ones who mixed the paint and not Jonathan. Oh, I'm so glad he's not guilty, Mandie. I just couldn't believe he would do a thing like that," Celia told her.

"It also means I have to ask Jonathan's forgiveness, and knowing him, he will really take advantage of that. I'll never hear the end of it," Mandie said with a sigh as she pushed back her tousled blonde hair.

"I don't know, he might not," Celia said.

"You know how he's always teasing me," Mandie said. "I think he enjoys it."

"That's because he likes you, Mandie," Celia said.

"Likes me? I don't think so," Mandie disagreed. "But I do really and truly hope he forgives me. I have been terribly wrong."

"Mandie, have you thought any more about what was going on back at the house?" Celia asked. "I mean, that no one was there, and all that food was prepared?"

"Yes, I have," Mandie said. "I don't understand it, though. We sure do run into some mysterious things, don't we?"

Celia smiled and said, "And you love it."

"I guess you're right, but I enjoy the mysteries back home even more. I understand the people better there," Mandie said.

"Well, a few more countries and we'll be on our way back home," Celia reminded her. "I think I'll be glad to get back and see my mother before I have to return to school."

"I will, too," Mandie agreed. "I miss my mother and Uncle John and my little baby brother. In fact, I miss everyone back in North Carolina."

"I wonder what time your grandmother and the senator will be back from town?" Celia asked. "They sure have been gone a long time."

"They said they didn't know exactly, but I imagine it will be in time for supper," Mandie said. "And this time we have stayed right with Uncle Ned. Grandmother should be happy about that."

"I wish everyone would hurry up and come back," Celia said.

"You know, we still don't know why the Chinese men, if they really are the ones who mixed the paint, have been tying up the miller and moving his windmill blades. How did they happen to get this far out in the country from the Delftware factory? Remember, it was a long way there," Mandie reminded her.

"Maybe they know he's working for the Dutch government," Celia suggested.

"Maybe, but why would they mess around with the windmill blades?" Mandie asked. "I sure hope Uncle Ned and Mr. Van Dongen catch those men and make them talk."

But she was disappointed as she looked up and saw her friends with Albert and his father coming toward them from the woods. The Chinese men were not with them.

"You couldn't catch them?" she asked Uncle Ned as he approached.

"Gone," the old Indian told her. He looked concerned, but said no more.

"Come, we will have more tea," Mr. Van Dongen told them, trying to sound hospitable.

The girls started toward the house and Jonathan, Ned, and Mr. Van Dongen followed.

Mandie wouldn't look directly at Albert because he was smiling at her, and she noticed that Jonathan was watching.

She couldn't quite understand why she felt nervous when Albert smiled at her. The feeling was all new to her. Ordinarily she would have just smiled back, but somehow she couldn't bring herself to do it.

Uncle Ned had gone into the kitchen with Mr. Van Dongen, and Mandie tried to sit away from Albert, but he followed her across the room and sat on a footstool near her chair. She still felt Jonathan watching, and this made matters worse.

Celia, knowing that Mandie was upset, spoke up to break the ice: "Where are you going to school in the United States, Albert?"

"Oh, to the Banham School for Boys in New York," he replied politely, hardly looking at Celia.

Jonathan said quickly, "That school is hard to get into.

You must have an awfully high academic score to make that."

"Top of my class here," Albert said with a shrug.

"Jonathan, if you stay home in New York and go to school, you and Albert may be able to see each other once in a while," Mandie said.

Jonathan frowned. "Maybe." Then he looked at Mandie and said, "I think I'd rather go to Chadwick's School for Boys in Asheville, North Carolina. That way I'd be near your school and could pester you and Celia now and then."

Mandie's mouth dropped open. She couldn't imagine Jonathan in school in North Carolina. She and Tommy Patton from the Chadwick School were good friends, and attended socials together. She didn't think the two would like each other.

"That school may be hard to get into, too," Mandie said coyly. "They're choosey, I understand."

"How choosey can they be? I'm number one in my class also," Jonathan said with a smirk.

That was hard to believe, but Mandie didn't think Jonathan would lie about such a thing. Number one, indeed. He must be awfully intelligent, but he had never showed off.

Albert asked, "Is this Mr. Chadwick's School special in some way? Should I also ask for entrance there?"

"Oh, no, no," Mandie told him. "It's not special at all. It's just a plain old boarding school for boys. You wouldn't like it. New York would be much better."

Mandie certainly didn't want Albert that close around. She felt her face flush as she saw Jonathan grinning at her. She turned her attention to Snowball in her lap.

"Then I will go to New York," Albert decided. "But I will have holidays when I could visit your town."

"In North Carolina we have very few holidays, and

then Celia and I always go home to visit our families," Mandie told him quickly. Changing the subject she asked, "Albert, why do you suppose the Chinese men have come around here? Did you know that they tied up your father and gagged him? And that they seemed obsessed with moving his windmill blades?"

Albert sobered and said, "My father told me what happened while I was away. Of course we would like the answer to your questions also. I will not be leaving again any time soon. We will catch them if they dare to return."

"I sure hope you do," Mandie said. "Your father told us he works for your government."

"Yes, and by the way, I do appreciate all the help you have all given my father."

Jonathan spoke up, "You know, we have a mystery to solve at the house where we're staying, too. All the servants disappeared this morning after Mandie's grandmother and the senator went to town. At noon there was food on the table, but no one was around anywhere."

"That is strange. Maybe I could give you a hand in searching them out," Albert offered.

"Oh, but we've searched the house inside and out and there's no one anywhere," Mandie quickly told him. She certainly didn't want him coming over to their house and following her around.

But she was anxious to get back and see for herself whether the servants had returned.

Chapter 12 / Surprise Events

Mr. Van Dongen once again served tea. He and Uncle Ned sat at one end of the room and discussed the events of the day. The young people talked on the opposite side. Mandie let Snowball down on his leash.

"You have a sister, don't you, Albert?" Mandie asked, knowing full well that he did.

"Yes, I do. She's at work right now," Albert replied.

"Did you know one of those Chinese men came to our house asking for her?" Mandie asked.

Albert looked shocked as he set down his teacup on a nearby table. "Asking for her? What did he say?"

Mandie turned to Jonathan for an answer.

"I went to the door, and he just asked if 'the lady' was there. And I said, 'What lady?' and he said, 'The lady from the mill,' so I assumed he was talking about your sister. I said, 'The miller's daughter?' and he said 'Yes,'" Jonathan explained.

"I have no idea what a Chinese man would want with

my sister," Albert said. He spoke across the room to his father and told him what Jonathan had said.

"She does not know any Chinese that I know of," Mr. Van Dongen said. "I don't understand."

"Understand what, Papa?" A girl opened the door to an inside hallway and stuck her head in.

"Come in, we have visitors," Mr. Van Dongen told her.

When the girl stepped into the room, a young man followed. Mandie gasped. They were the ones she had seen leave the parade, and later she had seen them at the parade by the Delftware factory.

"This is my daughter, Velda, and the widow De-Weese's son, Maurice," the miller said. "These are the visitors from the United States who are renting the van Courtlands' house."

Greetings were exchanged, and Mandie couldn't keep her eyes off the two. The daughter was beautiful and the young man was handsome. Mandie wondered about the times she had seen them.

"Velda and Maurice work for the flower parade commission," Mr. Van Dongen explained. "They are in many parades."

Mandie's thoughts were racing around the couple as the two sat down.

"We saw you in a parade the day we got here. We had to wait for it to pass before our carriage could go on. When I looked back, you all were leaving the parade and going back the other way," Mandie told them.

The two looked at each other. Then Velda said, "It might have been that we had to hurry to participate in another parade."

"And we saw you, Maurice, in the flower fields outside the house one night. You turned around and ran the other way," Mandie said.

"Oh, yes," Maurice admitted. "I was late getting home, and I didn't know who you were. I was in too big a hurry to stop and inquire. I'm sorry." When he smiled, Mandie noticed that he had perfect white teeth.

Albert spoke to his sister, "Do you know what has been going on here while I've been away?"

"Going on?" Velda asked.

"Yes." Albert's voice was sharp. "If you don't know, then where have you been?"

"I have been working," Velda insisted.

"Not twenty-four hours a day, certainly," Albert said. "While you were off fooling the time away, our father was tied up and gagged in the mill on two separate occasions."

Velda gasped. "What are you talking about?"

"You know very well that Papa is working with the government trying to find the person, or persons, who mixed the paint at the Delftware factory," Albert said. "Apparently two Chinese men may be responsible—"

"Chinese men?" Velda interrupted. Her face took on an ugly frown as she turned to Maurice. "Chinese men?" she repeated. "What do you know about this?" she asked him.

Maurice dropped his eyes and said, "Nothing whatsoever."

"One of the Chinese men came to our house looking for you," Mandie said.

"He did?" Velda said, incredulous. "Come outside," she said to Maurice. "I want to talk to you." She rose and hurried toward the door, Maurice behind her.

Once they were outside, Albert stood. "Please forgive me, but I must hear what is going on between my sister and Maurice."

"Yes, of course," Mandie said.

As soon as Albert had left the room, Mandie pinched

Snowball and made him meow.

"Oh, goodness," she said, "I have to take Snowball outside for a few minutes."

Jonathan grinned and Celia smiled. "I'll go with you," Jonathan said.

Celia added, "Me, too."

When they got outside, Velda and Maurice were nowhere in sight. Albert was standing in the yard, puzzled as to where his sister and Maurice could have gotten to so quickly.

Mandie let Snowball down on his leash. Then she caught a glimpse of Flour Rat coming out of the mill.

Albert went to pick him up. "We don't allow him to roam around outside," he said.

Suddenly, the four of them heard Velda and Maurice arguing inside the mill. "Exactly what are your Chinese friends up to?" Velda demanded.

"They are not my friends, you know that," Maurice was saying. "They are friends of friends of mine. They told me they wanted to use the windmill blades to signal to some other friends out in a boat as to where they were. That's all."

"That's all? And they came here and tied my father up. How dare you get involved in such a thing!" Velda was furious with him.

Albert stepped forward to make his presence known. Blocking the doorway, he asked Maurice in a threatening voice, "What is your connection with these Chinese men? You'd better tell me now or you'll have to tell the authorities later."

Mandie and her friends stood right behind Albert.

"How many times do I have to explain they are not my friends? They are friends of friends. That is all," Maurice said angrily, walking about inside the mill.

"You had better tell me if you know why those men tied up my father and left him here on two separate occasions," Albert demanded.

"Ask them yourself. They're right behind you," Maurice said matter-of-factly.

Everyone whirled around to see the two men standing behind them, this time with guns.

Celia swayed as if to faint, and Mandie quickly put an arm around her. Jonathan's eyes glittered with excitement, and Mandie knew he was going to try something brave.

Albert's face was seething with anger, and Velda was in shock.

"Inside," one of the men demanded as he waved his gun at Albert and the others. They all slowly moved inside the mill.

Maurice quietly slipped further into the mill. Mandie wondered whether he was preparing to rescue them when he had a chance.

"We will not hurt you if you cooperate. We only want to send a message on the windmill to our companions who will destroy the Delftware factory when we signal them."

Everyone gasped at his words. *So they were trying to send signals on Mr. Van Dongen's windmill for the factory to be destroyed,* Mandie thought. *What can I do about it? Mr. Van Dongen and Uncle Ned are still inside the house and don't know what's going on.*

"Why did you tie up my father?" Albert demanded as he advanced toward them, still holding the big gray cat.

Mandie instinctively knew what he was planning to do, and she walked to his side, holding Snowball.

"He got in our way," the smaller man said. Mandie noticed that both the men were smaller than Albert. But then Maurice, who had slipped back in with the young people, was a huge fellow, and who knew which side he was on?

"This time you are in *my way*!" Albert yelled at the man, at the same time tossing his cat in the man's face. Mandie threw Snowball at the other man, and both cats, excited and angry, clawed at the men's faces, causing them to drop their guns. Albert made a dive for the guns at the same time Maurice did, but Jonathan grabbed one of them first.

"Stop!" Jonathan demanded as Maurice grappled with Albert for the second gun.

When Maurice paid no attention to him, Jonathan fired the gun above everyone's head. At the same moment, an arrow flew through the open door and hit Maurice's hand. He fell to the ground, writhing in pain.

Mandie knew without looking that Uncle Ned had come to the rescue. Mr. Van Dongen rushed into the mill followed by the old Indian, and soon they had the two Chinese men tied up.

Velda stood back in anger, watching Maurice roll on the floor trying to remove the arrow. "You traitor!" she screamed at him, and then went running out into the yard.

Uncle Ned knew how to shoot an arrow and he also knew how to remove one. He bent down and worked to get the arrow out of Maurice's hand.

Mr. Van Dongen had his cart ready by then to take Maurice into town to the doctor, and then turn him and the two Chinese men over to the authorities.

Mandie moved close to Jonathan and said, "You sure know how to shoot a gun."

He frowned and said, "If I have to, I can, but I don't like to."

"If you know anything you haven't told us already, you had better speak up, for your own good," Mr. Van Dongen told Maurice as he helped him into the cart.

Maurice paused and said, "They have already sent the message. Everything inside the factory will be destroyed after the workers leave at six o'clock tonight."

"Six o'clock?" Mr. Van Dongen turned to Albert. "You must ride like your life depends on it and get the authorities to the factory in time. Go now!"

"Yes, sir," Albert said, turning to his horse still tethered nearby.

"I go, too," Uncle Ned said to the young man.

"Take one of our horses," Mr. Van Dongen said. "There's no time to get your own."

Albert was off, and Uncle Ned followed quickly on a horse from the Van Dongens' barn.

Jonathan spoke to Mr. Van Dongen: "I will ride into town with you to take these men."

Mr. Van Dongen hesitated and then said, "I believe you do know how to handle a gun. Get in." He handed Jonathan a gun to hold on the prisoners.

The girls watched in excitement as everyone left.

Mandie had picked up Snowball and was comforting him after his fright. Celia held Flour Rat.

Velda came out of the house just then and offered to take the cat so the girls could go. "I will take the cat inside. You two must go home now before it gets too late," Velda told them as she took Flour Rat from Celia and started toward the front door. "And thank you," she said.

"You're welcome. Goodbye," Mandie said, waving to the girl.

"We'd better hurry back to the house before your grandmother gets back," Celia told Mandie.

"Right. Let's go," Mandie said as she raced off through the flower fields.

When they arrived at the house, they entered through

the back door and found Gretchen in the kitchen.

"Well, I'm glad someone is here," Mandie remarked as she set Snowball down.

"I am sorry for what Anna did," Gretchen said to them as she stacked plates by the sink.

"Anna? What did she do?" Mandie asked.

"She got the meal ready, put it on the table, and then locked herself in her room while I was gone shopping and Dieter was off on an errand," Gretchen explained.

"But why did she do that?" Mandie asked.

"I apologize for her. She has never seen an American Indian before and she was afraid of him. She is always afraid of strangers," Gretchen said.

The girls looked at each other and laughed.

"If she only knew dear old Uncle Ned, she would love him," Mandie said. "Have my grandmother and Senator Morton come home yet?"

"Not yet, but I am preparing the meal," Gretchen said. "Anna has gone off to see a sick relative."

"We had some excitement just now over at the miller's house," Mandie told the maid.

Gretchen listened wide-eyed as she and Celia related everything that had occurred.

"Will your Uncle Ned be able to save the factory?" Gretchen asked.

"I think so. He always succeeds in time of trouble," Mandie told her.

"Mmmm. You young ladies wait in the parlor and I will bring you tea," the maid offered.

Mandie laughed and said, "Thank you, but we've already had tea twice this afternoon. We'll entertain ourselves until everyone gets back."

Not long after that, Mrs. Taft and Senator Morton returned. Mandie's grandmother was anxious to relate the latest news she had heard in town. The Dutch government was making an all-out search for the culprits who mixed the paint at the factory.

Mandie and Celia looked at each other and laughed. Mandie said, "Oh, but Grandmother, they've already been caught." She explained all that had transpired at the miller's house.

Mrs. Taft was shocked. It was hard for her to believe that the girls had been so closely involved in such a thing. "Oh, dear, I would have had a heart attack," she said. "I do hope Jonathan and Uncle Ned get back in one piece."

"I don't think we have to worry about either one of them," Senator Morton told her. "You go take a rest until it is time for supper."

"Yes, I suppose I should," Mrs. Taft said.

The girls also went to their room to discuss the exciting events of the day. In her mind, Mandie kept seeing Jonathan with that gun. He was so brave. She had falsely accused him, but it was real crooks who had been involved.

She wished the time would pass more quickly and that Jonathan would come back. Mr. Van Dongen dropped him off on his way to his own house, and when the girls heard Jonathan coming down the hallway, they ran out to talk to him.

"Tell us what happened!" Mandie demanded.

They found the sitting room on their floor and sat down. Jonathan shrugged his shoulders, grinned, and said, "We just took the three to the authorities. They put the two Chinese men in jail and accompanied Maurice to the doctor."

"Jonathan, I need to talk to you," Mandie began.

Celia knew they would want to be alone and quickly rose to leave. "I'll be back in a few minutes," she said, leaving the room.

Mandie looked straight at Jonathan and said, "I'm sorry. Please forgive me."

Jonathan grinned at her. "For what?"

Mandie took a deep breath and explained, "I falsely accused you of mixing the blue and the yellow paint at the Delftware factory. Please forgive me. I apologize with all my heart." She nervously twisted her hands.

"Mandie, you don't have anything to be sorry about. I didn't pay any attention to your accusation," Jonathan said. "I thought we knew each other well enough that we could say anything to each other without feeling bad about it. Just forget it."

"But I really have been mean to you, Jonathan, and I'm sorry," Mandie insisted. "I thought you were lying about your not being involved. I should have known better."

"All right, what do you want me to do about it? Kiss and make up?" He leaned forward teasingly and smacked his lips without touching her cheek.

Mandie moved backward and rubbed her cheek. "Jonathan! Be serious! If you have forgiven me, then we'll just talk about other things. Do you think Uncle Ned and Albert will get to the authorities in time to save the factory?"

"I'm sure they will," Jonathan said, sitting down again. "They can travel much faster on horseback than we could in the cart."

"I hope they're not gone too long. I can't stand waiting, not knowing," Mandie remarked. "By the way, Celia and I found out why everyone disappeared today." She told him what Anna had done and where the others had been.

Jonathan was amused by it all. By the time Celia came back into the room, Gretchen was announcing the evening meal.

Mrs. Taft decided they should not wait for Uncle Ned because he could be quite late getting back.

It was much later when he finally did return. Mandie, Celia, and Jonathan had waited up for him in the kitchen after the adults retired. When Uncle Ned came through the door they crowded around him.

"Everything fine now," he told them before they could bombard him with questions.

"And you must be hungry," Mandie said, going to the stove and opening the warmer. She quickly removed a tray of food that Gretchen had saved for him. She set it on the table nearby and the young people crowded around to listen to Uncle Ned's story while he ate.

"We got there, plenty of time," he told them, and then related how the authorities were able to thwart the destruction of the Delftware factory.

"And we got the Chinese men to jail," Jonathan said. "The authorities accompanied Maurice to the doctor, but he also was under arrest."

"I suppose this winds up our mystery here in Holland," Mandie said. "Grandmother says we'll be leaving shortly for Ireland."

"And Papoose will find mystery in Ireland, too," Uncle Ned said with a big smile.

"You always say that, Uncle Ned," Mandie told him. "How can you be so sure?"

"If no mystery, then Papoose make mystery," the old Indian said with a big laugh.

"But, Uncle Ned, I don't make up these mysteries. We always seem to run into them," Mandie said with a big smile, and then added, "I'm going to look real hard in Ireland, though, what with all those leprechauns I keep hearing about."